To Our Credit
(Two autobiographies)

By Peter Paul Saunders And Alex M. Saunders MD

Peter Paul Saunders   Alex M. Saunders, MD

Mr. Smith, from Venezuela

OK, I ADMIT it. I created Mr. Smith from Venezuela. Then I forgot all about him until my brother, Alex, reminded me a few weeks ago. You will find a complete description of Mr. Smith later, in a chapter including the important people in our story. For now, let me say he was created out of my imagination to deal with a potential deep crisis in the life of someone I loved. He was a distraction, aimed at being so complete that the crisis was averted. The strategy worked. I have to add that I did not think of it as a strategy at the time. I just knew something had to be done.

This time it is I who need to be distracted. And this book is thrown to me as a challenge for that purpose. How can I refuse?

PPS

Dear Reader,

The very short passage above is my words. But the challenge I threw to my brother is real. He accepted. I am quite amazed at how well it worked, and how much he wrote, (really dictated to his long time executive assistant, Trudy Weeks) in the last three months of his eventful life. He definitely needed a distraction. And what is a better distraction than to remember what is important in one's whole life, and to put it to paper. I helped, by proposing the idea. It may have been a help to see an outline, which he did not really follow. In honor of his memory and the serious effort he took in these last three months, I shall not edit one word of what he wrote.

In reviewing the outline months after Peter Paul passed away from pancreatic cancer, it occurred to me that it is, almost, a perfect outline for my own story as well. That is not because our accomplishments are the same. Not at all. And I claim no credit for his except in a very minor supporting role on a few occasions. Yet many of the things we did as youngsters we did together. And some were adventures in which we interacted so much that they form part of a common story. When you read the story of Mr. Smith from Venezuela you will understand how our lives interact. Not just two lives; an unusual family.

As for me, I would like to tell my story more by the people who influenced me most. They are a motley collection. Sadly, many of them are no longer with us. And with others, the contact was brief and incomplete. Likely, some did not think they had that much effect on me. I hope I do them justice in their brief mention that involves my "formation".

My plan in organizing this book is to place that part authored by Peter Paul right in the middle. Before that section is the story of my two brothers and I growing to a stage where our stories diverged. A few additions to Peter Paul's story follow his. Those comments are followed by the remainder of my story. That is the wise advice of my wife, Peggy, who is my long, long inspiration. And why not do it her way?

Although I am not a historian, I feel I should follow the rules. Any places where it is relevant I shall use the words of others that are available to me in a variety of paper sources. I shall also salt in some pictures, and pepper the pages with poetry to give some flavor.

There is a cartoon I once saw in a Catholic magazine. It was a man striding through the Pearly Gates with a large book under his arm. St. Peter, with a thin file open in his hands was looking down at a priest, also waiting to enter. The saint was saying, "The only thing I see here to your credit is that you never beat your wife."

The book you are about to read is to our credit.

AMS

Acknowledgements

Trudy Weeks was Peter Paul Saunder's long time executive assistant. She handled the toughest tasks for a demanding perfectionist with ease and grace. I recall being in their office on one occasion when Peter Paul asked her for a specific file by name. Her response was "I could get you that file if you really want it. But the file you need just now is already on your desk." That is how well Trudy knew my brother. Sadly, I must tell you I also told this story at Trudy's celebration and wake.

It must have been extraordinarily difficult for Trudy to take dictation daily for the preparation of this autobiography. I personally asked her to do so, and she felt it made good sense. No one else could have done what Trudy did. In addition to the record that she created, Trudy maintained Peter Paul in good cheer for the better part of his last few moths. I am so grateful to her.

My own daughter, Joanne Burns, proofread a good portion of my story. She took time out from another joint project to do this. Must have been fun, reading about her own birth and how her daddy missed the event. All the remaining errors in the book are mine, not hers.

My grandson Victor Saunders took the cover photographs at my son, Brian's wedding with my camera. They seem to be just right for this theme. All the other recent pictures are mine. I have no idea who took the remaining family pictures. They have been in the family for at least 70 years.

I have quoted several sources. None, to my knowledge are presently under copyright. My father's translation of the poem UGURTHA by HW Longfellow could have been followed by my re-translation from the Hungarian. Instead I chose to quote the Longfellow original.

I also quote several letters from now departed family members. These letters, or their originals before translations are all in my files. There is no way to recognize them except to cite who wrote them and when. This I do in my texts.

AMS

Table of Contents

Kids

OUR PARENTS WERE married in October of 1927. Their nuptial agreement was prepared by a most careful lawyer, our father. He was born in 1897 in Zagreb, then a part of Hungary, graduated from a highs school called Gymnasium and spent 3 ½ years in the Magyar Army during World War I. Immediately after the war, 1918, he went to university and graduated with a Doctor of Law degree. He joined the General Real Estate Bank of Hungary as a law clerk and grew rapidly to be the advisor to the board of directors and eventually became managing director of the bank. That is a position he held till 1937. With funds received as a dowry he invested in building apartment houses and was quite successful in the growth of a personal fortune. In 1937 he also invested in a factory making carding brushes for the wool carding industry. This was the only factory I knew and had visited. I never knew anything of our father's success. I only knew him as the respected head of the household with many servants, and a loving wife.

Our mother came from a family with considerable wealth. But as much as I want to investigate its origin now I have not been successful. I know that a year before our parents were married our maternal grandfather made an error of investment that may seem very large, but seemed not to bother him or his life style. He purchased an apartment house in Berlin. The family did not again see any of that investment until more than 80 years after its purchase. But that is an interesting story to be told later on. Mother, belonged to a strong willed family and likely was very glad to escape to her own house. I knew very little of that background when I was a child.

I was the third of three boys. My birth is marked in my father's third, or maybe fourth, book. It was a book of Hungarian and International Credit Law. In his introduction he mentions me and states that for him this was a time of waiting and of inactivity that he filled with writing the book. Thus, you see, I was in print almost before I was born.

As I gradually became aware of my surroundings I got to know two older brothers, two parents and a staff of what were called "servants" in a very large house. That was what I grew into, and I thought it was how it was in the world. I played with my brothers, and I talked with everyone in the house and in the garden and in the home above the garage that housed the Daimler. That is where the chauffeur and his wife lived; and the gardener also. Years later I could still hear my brother, Frank, quote the chauffeur, who in a drunken episode in his upper room set up a tirade about who was well dressed and who had "holes in their pants". And amazingly I can still visualize the man stumble around his room. By repetition, he taught me some words that I knew I dared no use in the big house. Had my parents known this story, the man would have not been our servant for very long.

Life for the first years revolved around a room that was nominally my own, but was shared with the governess who took care of the three of us. As Peter Paul says, this lady spoke no Hungarian, only German. I know that I saw the last of her in 1936, when she went back to Germany to vote. My father said, if she votes for Hitler she need not come back. That was a sign of the times.

Sándor Herschler
41. Jahre.

Sofie 37½ Jahre

1. Father as a young boy, with his parents (left) Grandmother, center, and uncles and aunts right. The framed picture is of our father's great grandfather.
2. Top Right, our mother's grandfather. Sándor is the Hungarian name the same as Alex. Taken about 1870.
3. Bottom Right, our mother's grandmother. The little girl in the picture is our Grandmother, Margit. Taken about 1870.
4. Bottom left our parent's wedding picture, October 1927.

My room opened on a terrace that stretched across the common bathroom between my room and my brothers' to the door at the room shared by Peter Paul and Frank. The terrace was the center of our life. Mother was almost always there, playing with us, reading stories. (I remember a translation of Jules Verne's travel to the moon.) She played the guitar just enough to lighten moods. And then she may send us out to play in the "garden" which was about 3 acres in back of the house. The front was out of bounds, with its formal lawns, rose trees and rock garden.

My room itself was very simple. Its only memorable features were the double pane windows which hinged separately to the inside and the outside. On the ledge between the two panes there was always a bottle of wine, and a glass. I rarely imbibed, but I knew it was there for me. A very large, old fashioned, ceramic heating fixture occupied a corner. I have seen these since only in old castles. I had a childish impression that someone, a dwarf in fact, could hide inside this structure and come out at night and hurt me.

The remainder of the house is not closely in my personal memory but I am privileged to have an array of photographs that speak for themselves. I am happy to share them with you. Please note the formal stairwell with that lovely banister where I so enjoyed sliding down, when the house was not full of guests. If we can grasp the size of the house it is no surprise in retrospect that, during the time of the Russian "liberation" our house was appropriated by the Russian generals as their headquarters.

But I do know of the family and extended family, who actively enjoyed this house and each other. My mother's mother, my grandmother Margit, frequently came and spent much time with us. She lived in the house next door. I remember as she would bathe us three boys together in the bath tub she told us a long story. It was a story of a family of three boys who had suddenly acquired a new baby sister. Their curiosity about the sister was so great that they jointly sneaked into her room pulled back the curtains to view her better and very strong sunlight was in her eyes. Ever since, she had suffered from poor eyesight. She was telling us her own story. I will speak of Margit much more later on, but please see the picture of her and her brothers as children on the next page.

1. Front of our house in Budapest.
2. Back of the same house
3. Library in the house.
4. Three brothers at back of house. Note the same ivy as in the picture above.

My father's parents also visited often and in the next picture you can see grandfather reading to three children from the simple book that is still popular in Hungary. The story of two monkeys called Muki and Bubu.

We three boys were inseparable until school started for my older brothers. There were tricycles, a sandbox, a puppy dog, a swing next to the sandbox. I personally took great pleasure in swinging high up above the sandbox and then let go, landing in the soft sand. Years later I found that it had very destructive effect on my knees. Both Peter Paul and Frank had knee and hip replacements later in life, so they must have had the same flying experience. It is one of those things that "you should not do at home". The governess should have been watching. I cannot remember how we got away with this trick but I know I did it very often. My dog's name was "Snowflake from Mayfair". That was a way to encourage us to think in English terms. But I just called him "Snowly".

I cannot say as much for Peter Paul, or for that matter for Frank either, but I got into a lot of disasters. And I was too young to think that they were not a way of life. There is only one more I wish to tell you about at this time. It included Tommy.

He was a cousin, Tommy Horvath, some twelve years older than I, who lived in the same apartment building where my mother lived while in downtown Budapest. 17 Vaci utca (street). He came to visit us on the day that my Uncle Stephen got married. We played out in the gardens close to the swings. Tommy suggested a game of knights, where he put Frank on his shoulders, Peter would put me on his shoulders, and there was to be a battle. But I lost my balance the first time I mounted, fell backwards and hit my head. There was a lot of blood but no serious injury. Mother remained by my bed for the next hours with a great demonstration of concern. It was many years later I learned, from Tommy, that it was an excuse for mother not attending her brother's wedding, because she disapproved of it. Did I say already that mother had good judgment?   I shall tell you about Irma a little later on.

On very few occasions I also visited with Uncle Leopold (Lipot,

Leo) and his wife, my Aunt Ella. In looking back over the times, and reading family correspondence and even newspaper stories, I conclude that he was sort of the family leader in Budapest. I only mention him here because my memory of him from my childhood is that his dog, a dachshund, bit me in a fit of temper. Soon after that Lipot left Budapest. He and Ella were the first of the family to migrate to Vancouver, Canada. Migration is the subject of the next few chapters. I will put it into more context than I remember from that time. Unlike most historians I read, I shall forgo political judgments. Rather look at it all from the eyes of a young boy.

That young boy also remembers grand dinner parties, both in our parents house and elsewhere with family. Just to mention a few, there was a dinner party for a Cardinal Pacelli who was visiting from Rome. I have no idea why he visited our house, but I remember his name from that time. There was also a dinner party at my Grandmother Szende's house. Her mother, my great grandmother, was there, as were many uncles and aunts and cousins. My personal trick at this dinner was to drink all the wine put in my glass. When a tiny bit more was put in the glass, I drank it also and then stated that my glass had dried out. I think I learned the comment from my grandfather who enjoyed the joke as much as I.

Family at large

JUST FOR A few lines now, let me tell about former generations. Almost all of this comes from writings of other people and I decide here to let them speak for themselves. That is, because these others from time to time had answered questions from me or Frank in our later lives. The first is from Eva Martin, who is my father's cousin. Some of it is a translation form Hungarian.

Dear Frank,

You probably will be surprised that I am answering your letter of October 12, 84. I went to visit Mickó in Jacksonville last week and she gave me your letter to answer it, because unfortunately she is not well and is unable to answer it. ....

Now I would like to answer your question about our family, going back in time. You remember OMAMA, our dear grandmother, and your great grandmother. Her name was Karolina (nicknamed: Linka). Her husband, our grandfather and your great grandfather was Jozsef Gutfreund. He was a darling man, a great man, I remember him very well. I got my first spiritual teaching from him, sitting on his lap. He was director of a railroad company, that time in Hungary. He was a Free-Mason. I still have his Masonic emblem, a beautiful silver star, denoting his tenth anniversary as a free-mason, his name is engraved on it and

Deák Ferenc Lodge, the date 1890 – 1900. .... He was born in Nyitra, Hungary, son of a teacher. His father was married three times,. There was one son by the first marriage but he died at and early age. No children from the second wife, and Jozsef was born from the third wife. Also a brother named Simon, who lived in Komron, and never married.

Now about our dear Omoma and her family. She was born in Pécs in 1854. Her maiden name was Sachs. And I know her mother's maiden name was: Eisler. Fanny Eisler. Omama's father was Jakob Sachs. He lived to 104 years. He would have lived longer, but when his wife, Fanny, died, who was much younger than him he refused to eat and died within a week. Once Omama showed me a clip about her father's death. He was a well know man in Pécs, a builder. And it said in the article that he was the oldest man in Pécs. They lived before my time, but I remember their photograph hanging on the wall. ------

We all lived happily until Nazism showed up on the horizon. Omama died of starvation, at age 92, in a Nazi concentration camp, set up in Budapest, where they dragged her from her home, together with your grandparents, Sárika and Henry, and also the Vikárs, Tücsök and Jancsi. I myself got there also with my son, Andy, who was at that time one year old. We were all set up in a small room with five other people, all together 12. All windows were broken, and the temperature was below 0. No electricity, no gas, no water. No food except for a bean soup a day which was only a few beans in water. I was still nursing Andy, otherwise he would have died of starvation. We slept 6 of us in a double bed. We went to bed at 5 in the afternoon when it started to get dark. We never undressed, because we never knew what will happen. The Nyilas's (Hungarian Nazi Party. The word means like an arrow.) constantly came and executed people or dragged away, shooting them into the Danube. The siege of Budapest was going on and we heard constant bombing and gunfire. This is where our dear Omama died on December 24, 1944. That day was Andy's first birthday. Finally the Russians liberated us on January 16, 1945.   Eva (Martin)

Please note that all the direct family in the tree described by Eva are in the picture. My Great Great Grandfather's picture is on the wall behind the group. And there, in the front, is my father as a youngster.

A second source is Juan Tomas Horvath. Yes, this is Tommy who, with his father, Ernö, had visited Buenos Aires. Later he migrated there and I corresponded with him there much later. Ernö was Uncle Leo's brother. Hence Juan Tomas Horvath was our third cousin. But he lived as a child in the same apartment house as my mother and her brother, our Uncle Stephen. Here is his account of my mother's side of the family.

January 1999

Dear Alex:

First of all: I am awfully glad to have found you and even more happy to see your interest in our family history.

First question: is it a national or a family trait that makes us so direct. I think, Alex, both of them. My late Father was tremendously outspoken (a trait I inherited) and that always brings more enemies than friends. People like to be cajoled and don't like to hear: "you ---".
(Pardon!) Horváth Sándor és Fiai (and sons) began as a store and much later became a factory in which Gábor, Kriszti's father and I worked. Together with another company they founded a third chemical industry, (zinc oxide and red lead) which, after the war, became my responsibility. (Smelting Metallurgical & Metal Works Ltd.)

As for Margit's and Joanne's eyesight problems: you are the geneticist and should know better than anybody. I really doubt they could have had such a strong light as to harm a child's eyes. They were poor people. Alex: Sándor, your great grandfather and with your name, died in 1918 of diabetes, months before insulin had been discovered and I was born in 1919. I never knew my paternal Grandparents. Sándor had the reputation of a "Schöngeist", someone seeking the beauties of life or in life and decidedly was no businessman. Sophie, my Grandmother was a very pretty but also energetic woman, they say, and after all the stories delivered to me, it was the two brothers who took over the business quite young, mainly to permit Lipót to study at the University.

I received from Kriszti a picture with Sándor at the left and Sophie with her 4 children .It should be the same you mention. You are again a 100% right: after my Father's death my uncle Jenö (Lily's dad) found a pleasure in saying: you are the typical third generation, unable to build up something, wanting only to spend the money produced by your elders. Yes, fortunately, life proved him wrong.

I cannot answer your question if a poet can be a businessman! Sándor was a poet.   I was a businessman until 1989 and in October 1995 I started all of a sudden writing poems.(I shall send you some.) I should say there is no incompatibility whatsoever, only I didn't exercise both simultaneously.

Subject: EVA, my beloved wife.

As already told: she was 15 I was 17 when on a private party we fell in love. It is lasting now since that day, almost 64 years, thanks to the Almighty.

You know that on March 19 1944 Hitler invaded Hungary. It was the worst time to marry. But as the Germans had the wonderful habit of taking unmarried girls from the street to take them to soldier's brothels, it were my future In Laws who asked my mother   (I was in the Army) if she would mind me to marry Eva, considering that we anyway intended to do it at some later date. My Mother was against. Of course I said yes. Until the day before the wedding my mother tried to dissuade me. Why? Because the Hevesi family was not good enough for her darling son, who deserved at least a royal princess.

Well, I requested license and got a whole of five (5!) days to marry. Eva and a civilian dress, I in uniform were married in a side chapel of Budapest's Cathedral (called Bazilika), on May 1ˢᵗ, 1944.. After five days I had to go back and Eva went back to her parent's house, but already with a wedding ring. (5 gr was the maximum permitted, inside hollow. We still wear them and will until death does us apart.)

The next time I found a subterfuge to go to Budapest I went straight to her house – and found it 100% bombed out, in ruins. It so happened, that the beautiful villa on Gellért mountain, having a splendid panorama on the Buda mountains, the Royal Castle, the Danube, etc. has been taken unceremoniously by no less than the Supreme Commander of the occupying German Army. This, of course, the Russians knew and it became a special target for their bombers and they fulfilled their duty.

Must have got a medal for it. I, of course, must have thought that my young bride was buried underneath. Nevertheless I went out to seek her (10 a.m.) and with God's help found her safe and sound at 6.p.m. in the house of friends. Great was my relief. But at 7 p.m. I had to tell her that at midnight I have to be back at my unit.

That was the beginning of our married life!

Eva also had her "baccalaureate" but in those times thought it better to study something she could use within a short time. So she studied textile drawing (not fashion drawing, something quite different.) Drawings for silk or cotton manufactured for dress making. She insisted on having it written into our marriage license. From then on, she never ever made a single design...

My Father in Law was, as already told, a very wealthy man, CEO of one of Hungary's big textile industries and had said to my mother, that never in life shall I have financial problems.

But, to my luck, in every sense of the word, I wanted Eva for a wife and not the money. My father in law still managed to put my name on the board of directors of the company before his unexpected death. The company had been "nationalized" by the communist government, but, against all logic, they offered a small house inside the factory premises to her, which she accepted, as her house was a ruin.

The Germans, in the middle of an enormous ring formed by two Russian Armies (Marshalls Malinovsky and Tolbuchin), in their rage had exploded all Danube bridges. One under full traffic, with trams, buses, cars and people. When the Russians managed to repair in a provisory way one of the bridges only for use by foot, Eva undertook the risky excursion with a rucksack on her back to what used to be her house. THERE SHE FOUND IN PERFECT ORDER TWENTY GOLD BARS OF 1 KG each!!! She brought them back, under tremendous danger. My Mother in Law took them (by foot, approx. 20 km) to her little house inside the factory. The good willing manager ordered the house to be painted anew. One of the painters lifted the rucksack and found it suspicious for its weight and denounced it. The so called " Economic Police" promptly came and confiscated it all for the State. They gave a receipt...

Thanks God I had married the girl and not her money!!!

Juan Thomás Horváth

Note, over more than a year of correspondence, Tommy gave me a very broad family history in his colorful mix of Hungarian, German and Argentinian phrases, all attempting to be English. They are not all relevant to this story and so I only include here episodes that deal with episodes around the times in Hungary that we three brothers had no opportunity to observe. We could have had similar adventures had our father not taken a difficult decision that I shall next portray.

(Not Family at all)

On doing some research on our family tree I accidentally found a familiar name, Szende Pál. Although our father shares the name I now understand why he uses Peter and Paul together consistently. Paul Szende was born in Nyirbártok in 1879. The only similarity to our father was that he also studied law and practiced for a while in Budapest. He became a (1900) founding member of a political society that changed character over time. At first it was liberal and intellectual. It was called the Society for Social Science. (Better translated as the Society for Social Knowledge). This society split in 1914 and he became a founding member of the Hungarian Bourgeoise Party. In 1918 at a time of revolution he became a member of the Karolyi government and eventually the Minister of Finance. That government was short lived. It dissolved in March of 1919, and Szende Pál fled to Vienna and later to Rumania, where he died in 1934. During his very short popularity a street was named for him, as it happened, very close to the apartment where our mother's family lived. I show that street sign in a picture, but it is definitely not named for our family.

Foreign Travel.

Every summer, and sometimes in the winter as well, our parents and we three boys went on vacations in other countries. There was a lake in Italy, at Cortina, a ski resort in Austria that I do not remember by name, a city vacation in Portugal, to name a few.

At my age of 8, it was not surprising to find us traveling through Vienna, Austria, to Zurich, Switzerland. In Vienna we stopped for a meal, and found ourselves on the main boulevard, where we watched a very large army contingent marching, really goose stepping, right down the center of the street. Looking around I saw, and perhaps felt, fear in the eyes of other spectators.

I honestly do not remember the rest of the summer. Just that at some time we met with Uncle Stephen and Aunt Irma as well, and there was much talk that I did not fathom. At first they did not have their plans complete. Stephen decided later that he was going to travel to a far away place. Vancouver, I found out later. And there was much talk about how they all could try to persuade Margit to join the trip. That part was not successful.

Late in the summer I found out that we were not going home to Hungary. There was had no explanation. We were going to a small town called Freiburg to be in school. None of us had problems with the German language in school. One memory was that one night I woke up and asked my father for half an apple, in German!

It was in Freiburg, also that I learned about how babies are made, and how they are born. My mother was walking with the three of us in a late afternoon, and explained it all to us. She did an amazingly good job and seems that she was pleased that she was able to fill this parental obligation. I know that much of this was also on her mind because I heard her complain about pain in those parts of her body. But I cannot remember all the anatomical terms.

Within a week from that teaching episode, our mother was dead. I suspected, but never knew for sure until I had my correspondence with Tommy years later, that she had somehow taken her own life. And the reason for it is still obscure.

I have pieced together an extraordinary tale from memory, and a lot of surprisingly well preserved papers. My father had never expected to return to Hungary. In the next few months he traveled a lot to put things in order. He went back to Hungary and apparently sold his holdings in his factory. Also must have liquidated much more of his holdings. He also was in correspondence with business associates in London and in Australia, and perhaps many other places, attempting to make a future for himself. I have a letter responding to his from the president of a carding brush factory in New South Wales, informing that the business was not big enough for father to invest and become a director. Another letter from London that insisted that we all come to England regardless of any financial capability. A most beautiful letter saying we would be sponsored by this man's business.

During this time, we three boys were in a boarding school in a beautiful setting in Sant Gallen. It all seemed so natural to me to be in school, and in a routine life, that I surely did not know the heroic effort of planning and our father's accomplishment in those few months.

He evaluated a large number of possible business opportunities, with a focus on a profitable enterprise he could either join or develop in Australia. Some if his correspondence, at least the responses to his queries and advertising are still available to read.

He also received proposals from a variety of inventors to develop new products with them. The most interesting of these was one that produced artificial horn, like the horn of a bull, from Casein, the protein of milk. This inventor described a formable material that he had already manufactured in Ireland, and the Irish corporation gave him strong positive recommendations. In retrospect I do not know why father did not pursue this further. It now seems like a precursor of the plastics industry and would have had a strong market at that time.

On what I first thought was a routine visit from father, we were told the plan. We are all to go by car to Genoa, Italy, and board a ship to sail to Australia, and settle there and go to school in a place called Melbourne. I did not understand all that was going to happen. Simply I accepted that father had a plan, and shall start the next day.

The Daimler had disappeared. In its place there was a sleek Alpha Romeo sedan. It was much more compact than our first car. And it was the first time I ever remember father himself driving a car. We drove over the Alps and raced across northern Italy on roads that we would be ashamed to travel now days. But that is all there was.

In Genoa I recall walking around in the City on arcade-like sidewalks, all in the shadows, and trying to communicate in a language none of us really knew. It turned out that the ship had sailed about two hours before we arrived in the city.

> Are there any psychiatrists reading this story? Well let me witness for them a reality we often hear about. I had totally forgotten about those sidewalk arcades. But for years, as an adult I had this dream about walking on those arcades and then getting lost in some city, with streets I did not recognize and streetcars whose destination I could not guess. But I knew I had to decide and take one of these street cars! Sometimes bizarre things happened when I did take that ride. Well, years later I was giving a scientific paper to a genetics conference in Genoa. And I

saw the arcade as I walked around the old city. And then the dreams just stopped.

We still had the car. Racing back across the northern part of Italy and over to Zagreb. I do not know how father managed to get us aboard an airplane that night. And so we traveled to Athens. On the way I had a chance to look out the window of the Foker Tristar passenger plane and observed a beautiful series of flares. I was fascinated and watched enthusiastically. Later, someone told me that those were anti-aircraft shells bursting all around us. Someone was trying to shoot us down. How lucky that the gunners were so poorly trained at the start of the conflict!

In Athens we had a wait of several days. How interesting that even in periods of stress father decided to use the time to our benefit. He took us to see the Parthenon. Those old buildings on top of the hill were impressive even to a nine year old. But more fun to run up and down the marble steps than to examine the architecture in detail. I did so, enthusiastically and even fell and skinned my knee right there on the bottom steps of the Temple of Athena.

We also went to a good restaurant. It was my birthday, March 29, 1940, and I was 9 years old. The waiter tried to embarrass me by presenting me with a menu with Greek letters. I simply told him I am too young to read, so he told me what the fare was. And everybody else listened and was able to order without anyone being further stressed.

In those days when one traveled by air, everyone was weighed so as not to overburden the aircraft. I was able to contribute my light weight to the average. And we were off on a Dutch, KLMN, plane that hoped form Athens to Alexandria, to Jerusalem and then on to Rangoon, Pacific Islands and finally arrived in Darwin on April 8. We actually stopped in Darwin to have lunch at the airport. It was soup that I did not like. Yet when someone asked me if I would like some more, I made the mistake of saying "Please?" Which is a translation of the Hungarian word for "please repeat you question." But the result was; I got to eat more soup!

With a few more stops we arrived at Melbourne. And I have to confess that I remember not one feature of that city. Nevertheless a lot happened to us in that city.

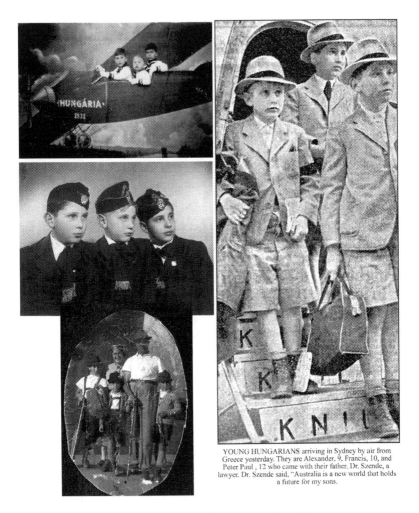

YOUNG HUNGARIANS arriving in Sydney by air from
Greece yesterday. They are Alexander, 9, Francis, 10, and
Peter Paul , 12 who came with their father, Dr. Szende, a
lawyer. Dr. Szende said, "Australia is a new world that holds
a future for my sons.

Three brothers Early photos. The composite with parents was
taken in Switzerland in 1939.

Melbourne

ONCE MORE THE routine developed of going to school, and returning to the boarding house where father had set up rooms. The routine was somewhat expanded because our mastery of English was poor. I had only one year of school taught English reading, in Budapest, at the English Hungarian School. So father, in his wisdom hired a tutor to help each of us develop our skills as fast as possible. Mrs. Foster was very good. I actually do not remember a transition to speaking English within the very first months in Melbourne.

During this time in Melbourne father was busy trying to develop a new business venture. He also was in contact with Vancouver. In the letters that Peter Paul had preserved all this time I read a response from Uncle Leo that was very encouraging and gave solid suggestions, but also said that it was not a good time to come to Vancouver, since his Ella had just developed a severe illness and had passed away.

I will now stop my narrative briefly and include here a letter sent by John Mendel to Uncle Leo and Uncle Stephen. I translate this from German. John Mendel was a distant cousin who lived in Sydney. This will be followed immediately by a letter from Uncle Leo to John Mendel.

Report on the demise of Pali.

As the Children came home from school on Saturday, they found their door, as always, locked, and as their father did not respond to knocking, went to the owner of the boardinghouse and asked her to unlock the door and to call a doctor. Because it was dinner-time and for other reasons the doctor first came 4 ½ hours later and found Pali unconscious under the influence of sleeping medicine. He was taken to the hospital and everything was done to save him but he died unfortunately on Sunday, ___ without regaining consciousness. He left two farewell letters in which I give the original text.

> *To my children:*
>
> *My sweet, dear children. I brought you over to the land of promise. You should be good and respect God and you should be happy. Your dear mother and myself will keep eyes on you from heaven. God be with you. Your father.*

And one addressed to Mrs. C Forster 46 Cochrane Street Brighten 85 Victoria, Australia, Dear Mrs. Forster,

> *I believe I fulfilled my paternal duty bringing my children to this excellent country. I cannot live longer, my nerves are ruined. Please take care of my children and my fortune, which belongs, of course, to my children. I am awfully obliged to you.*

Mrs. Forster was the English tutor for Pali and the children, an especially nice and honest lady with three children. Pali asked her on Friday afternoon, that if he was sick she would take the children, and if she could deal with that in case anything happened to him. She did not answer anything formal to him. But Pali repeated himself several times, but said it is not relevant in the short time. But there was nothing in writing and there is no witnessed document. It was assumed that there was no will and that there was to be a Public Trustee appointed. The Public Trustee can then begin to establish what to do, and when it is agreed, that there is no will then something can proceed. Since the public

Trustee was not paid for work Public Trustee ???assigned it to a private Trustee Company. By regulation the Trustee is awarded 2 ½ % interest to operate.???? Over this (decision) no one established that after the interest any funds could be called for.

> *From Uncle Leopold I got this cable:*
>
> *I am the Szende Orphans only available nearest relative. Wish John and Edith Mendel to be appointed orphan's trustees guardians. Only available relatives sent letter expressing same. Wish please secure efficient lawyer put children in good class boarding school. –*

(Broad translation) there is confusion resulting form local decisions and a directive and decision form a foreign land in English. It was decided that John and Edith Mendel are to be the Trustees. This pleased everyone and it is considered that Pista (Stephen) will eventually be nominated Guardian. At any rate it is possible to dispense funds in the meanwhile. A lawyer is appointed who is _____. In Sidney.

And so we arrived in Sydney within a few days.

Just a few details to complete what happened. An Australian Trustee company was indeed appointed. There was close to 3/4 mm Australian Pounds which in those days was a considerable sum. The Trustee was to be in charge of the funds and provide allowances to permit our welfare and hand over the remainder at our age of 21 years. In addition, our father's estate that still remained in Hungary was essentially divided among the surviving relatives in Budapest. They included the apartment house and other investments. One item that was not sold was the original house that I remember as my first home. It was kept as an investment because it was considered that its value could increase greatly after the years of war ravaged Budapest recovered. That never happened. The Russian Generals recognized its value and simply took it over.

Sydney and Riverview College

JOHN AND EDITH Mendel were a marvelously well adjusted couple. They accepted three youngsters in their home in spite of having never had any children. These were lively children who had to learn a bit more English but were otherwise into everything, and in three different directions, always. Edith directed some of my energy into helping with the dishes, because she saw that I marveled at the suds in the dishwater. I even had taken some dishwater and made more suds with the hand held egg beater.

We lived with the Mendels a brief time, and John followed Uncle Leo's directive and had us enrolled in the best boarding school nearby. The Mendel home was at Mosman Beach. From there we always went by Ferry to Riverview. The school is actually called St. Ignatius College, Riverview.

There are several things to note about our stay at Riverview. First, we did a fair bit of traveling back and forth to the Mendel home. During these trips by ferry, it became obvious that Peter Paul was in charge! He accepted the responsibility. In many ways, he has felt responsible for Frank and me ever since. And I, for one gave him the respect that that deserved.

The other thing that happened, of course is that each of the three of us, now separated in classes and in dormitories, began to develop our own personalities. This was bound to happen even though we got together very often, especially while Hungarian was still a language that gave us some comfort. Very likely we overlooked how superb a school Riverview really was. The Jesuits indeed establish a discipline for both study and achievement. Sports were not emphasized, but were a strong part of the program and everyone had to take part. I still have the tiny silver cups that I won for footraces on Sports Day. And we all had to take part in musical performances. For example there was a performance of the Samuel Tailor Coleridge's Ancient Mariner in three part harmony. It would be difficult to forget the poem after all the rehearsals we did. And sometimes I still fall asleep at night while reciting it silently to myself.

Riverview had a most beautiful Chapel. It was larger than many churches I have been in. There were complete Missals in the pews for every student. In those days the Missals were arranged with the Latin text on one side and the English text on the other side of a two column page. The idea was that we should learn the Latin from being able to read the English. For me I essentially learned both at the same time by gradually learning the context. There was plenty of repetition, every day. But for me it was the time to learn the languages. And I was never bored.

Then for a while, since John and Edith Mendel spoke German at home, we became reasonably proficient in all three languages.

In the background John Mendel and our family in Vancouver began a communication. At its conclusion, some 18 months later, we were told, (not asked) that our new home will be in this mysterious, far away place. We could not even pronounce its name. The "ou" became two syllables, until that was corrected for us after our arrival.

And so, with Peter Paul in charge, three boys aged from 11 to 14 years old boarded a KLM Klipper in Sidney and went off to New Zealand. There we had a week's wait to catch the next Klipper that island hopped to San Francisco. And that trip also took about a week. Auckland, New Zealand was a fun place. We had a hotel room with one giant bed. As you can imagine, it soon became a trampoline. We did quite a bit of sight seeing.

Indeed we saw the local geographical marvel, where two inlets from opposing sides of the big island come very close together. As the tide comes in on one side, it is going out on the other. Yes there are some very confusing places in the world, but for three young adventurers it was a matter of accepting what is. And that lesson we learned as youngsters without guidance from adults.

In the Canton Islands, the third stop, we were encouraged to snorkel under the bow of the seaplane. The water was so clear that we could see fish swimming yards below, in the shadow of the plane.

In Honolulu, the fourth stop, we were taken in charge by a steward form the plane. He drove us on a site seeing tour in a car that had a special knob on the steering wheel for making rapid turns. It saved our lives because the Steward had to make a rapid turn to escape a collision with an oncoming car. One remembers small details for unknown reasons. For example, I remember that we only had two beds in the hotel room and so Frank decided he was going to sleep in the bath tub. Being a warm night that may have been the best choice. At any rate, there was no one to tell us that he could not do so. Had we gone through Hawaii three weeks later, likely we would all have died. The date we left was October 15, 1941.

The flight from the big Island took 19 hours. There were beds arranged on the Klipper. It was not at all hard to sleep. And I have often since been able to go to sleep on a plane before it even takes off.

And so we were met on the San Francisco water front at the seaplane port by Uncle Stephen. Peter Paul was willingly relieved of his command. And we flew by regular plane to our new home in Vancouver.

I Nearly Died!

"When I was a child," I could say to you,
"I thought like a child." But it's not true.
It's not worth writing in pen and ink
Because, you see, I did not think.
I
Imagine a vacation spot, serene,
Where the skies are blue, the water clean,
And mountains rise right out of the lake.
It's the type of place **where** parents take
Little children. Here they can play
While everyone rests on a holiday.

Imagine a lakeside swimming enclosure
Constructed of wood, It let through the water.
It held children in a shallow place.
I recall this setting, my first disgrace.

The top of the crib was of solid wood.
I could walk on it. My balance was good.
My brother, Peter, my father and I
Walked out and watched the fish swim by.

The fish seemed tame, they were white and gold.
They must have been carp. I was three years old.
I stepped to the edge to look closer. I fell.
I just had time to let out a yell.
Just as I splashed, in fear, I could feel
My brother hold me by one heel.
The fish did not move. They were really tame.
My brother held on till my father came.

I say to my brother, Peter, who
Saved me from drowning. I thank you.

II

When I was four, that winter we
Traveled to a resort to ski.
Of course I was then very small
And could not keep up with others at all.

There I was on my stubby skis,
Poles and gloves, warm BVDs,
Slipping and sliding close by the hotel.
I don't know how many times I fell.

But no one was watching. I tried many things.
I developed some skill. Oh what joy that brings!
 And developed some balance while sliding on snow.
It's easier turning, the faster you go.

I trudged up the hill and came down even faster.
What other challenges could I really master?
And here I come to my second disaster.

Before the hotel the road was a sight.
A bus and some cars, the snow was packed tight.
It looked like faster skiing was there,
So I went on the road. I would go anywhere!

Slipping, and sliding. I was scared just a bit.
I skied up behind the bus in a minute.
Put my pole on the bumper and rested it there.
The bus started forward. That gave me a scare.

My pole was stuck on the bumper, tight.
On my wrist, too. Boy, what a fright!
Sliding on skis, first. Then on my face.
Rolling, spinning, we went quite a pace.

At a corner we stopped. I could still not free
My pole from the bus. Then a mailman saw me.
He ran after the bus, somehow got me off,
Then away from the road. Then he started to laugh

Then he swore at me. I had never heard
A faster racing of word upon word.
His anger was very hard to ignore.
Then he left me there. I saw him no more.

To that unknown mailman. I say to you;
For saving my immature life, I thank you.

III

By the time I was 8 years old
It was not unusual for me
In the summer to be told
"Once more we leave Hungary"

Every summer and winter we
Traveled where it is good to ski
Or swim, or hike. Whatever
One does in best of weather.

There was some danger in travel
Though the War had not yet begun.
The world did not yet unravel.
For me it was time to have fun.

It is difficult to recall
How, when the War had begun,
We did not return in the Fall.
By now we were on the run.

My mother mentioned some pain,
Though mostly she kept it inside.
She never saw home again.
It was Switzerland where she died.

There was no time for grieving.
No time to know one's mind.
I just knew we were leaving,
Leaving it all behind.

Next my father, two brothers and me
Were racing by car through Italy
To Genoa. Speed limits ignored.
But the boat sailed an hour
Before we could board.

Retracing our steps, I can still recall,
We arrived in Zagreb by nightfall;
Boarded a German Fauker Tristarr.*
The fare being traded in for the car.

Out the window, I was aware,
Every few minutes I saw a flare.
They were beautiful.
How could I tell
That each was an anti-aircraft shell?

And so we escaped, by devious travel
A war that caused the world to unravel.
The boat that sailed with four passengers less
Was   bombed   and   sank,   while   passing   Suez.

My gratitude seems to be very small:
To my father, who predicted it all.
A brave man in trouble, steering a wheel
Through war torn Europe with nerves of steel.

I thank the untrained gunners, who
Missed the plane in which we flew.
And here is another you can quote;
I thank God we missed that boat.

III 1/2

In case you think it coincidence,
To go on with my reminiscence,
My brothers, Peter, Frank and me
Spent a day in Hawaii.

That was in 1941.
Precisely, it was December 1.
We missed a big one! So I pray,
Thanks, every Pearl Harbor Day.

Vancouver 1

ESL *
Let me tell you a story
Before memories decline.
I am not looking for glory,
But, yes, the story is mine.

Three brothers escaped from the hell of war
Their ages ranged from eight to eleven.
They traveled alone and traveled far
While their parents went off to Heaven.

They found an uncle, who took them in.
What else could he do?
It would have worked, except that
His wife was a shrew.

So he sent them off to boarding school
With good luck as a wish.
That would have worked, except that
They hardly yet spoke English.

So they began to learn, but now and then
Spoke their own language between them.
That would have worked, except that
The other children beat them.

The others, you see, thought it strange
That someone spoke another language.
The three boys looked at what was in store
And maturely decided; nevermore.

Nevermore to be caught as strange.
Their own language ended.

Except when others were out of range.
In language, at least, they blended.

Well, there were other strange little boys.
They suffered just as much.
One was shell shocked, one full of hives,
One nearly blind, and such.

Each was attacked, if not by fist,
Then mentally they were broken.
Children are cruel. You get the jist?
Well, our English became well spoken.

I was the youngest of the three.
Here is how it affected me.
It helped me to understand
Strangers in a strange land.

*   English as a second language.

Vancouver 2

In Vancouver we joined a family that had arrived some years before. That family consisted of our Uncle Leo, Uncle Stephen and his wife, Irma. Uncle Leo was nominally retired. He had made some careful investments in apartment houses in Vancouver when he first arrived, and these gave him a fair income. He lived modestly in a house just off Cambie Street and 27th avenue. There was a house keeper, who was not memorable. In fact there may have been a series of house keepers and I would not have known or remembered. Having been a successful bank owner and manager in Hungary, he was a strong person, but very lonely. Thus he worked hard to keep the family together by making certain that we actually got together at least weekly. His small house became a common meeting ground for whenever any of us were in Vancouver on a Saturday for lunch.

For people young enough to be in the work force Canadian law provided an obligation to spend the first five years either in the lumbering industry, or on a farm. Hence Uncle Stephen, who was not really in the work force any time before (he was trained as an international lawyer) decided he would buy a farm. This farm was some distance from Vancouver, in Ladner. It was at first some 80 acres. And later he bought another 40 acres some distance from the first piece.

It was a dairy farm. The acreage mostly supported the milk cows and everything else was incidental. Thus there was a good crop of hay. Oats were grown for the straw that was bedding for the cows while in the barn. And peas were a secondary crop. The vegetable went to the local cannery, while the pea vines were harvested into a giant silo in the fall and became food for the cows all winter.

Since Stephen had no experience in farming he did two very opposing things. He hired as a consultant the agriculture professor at University of British Columbia on an occasional visit. He also hired an excellent farm foreman. The foreman, Walter, was an impressive person. He was completely dedicated to the farm. He was completely capable, in both planning the yearly cycle of activity and also in maintenance. At one time I heard him say that there was nothing on the farm that he could not fix. Often I saw him making his own parts for the tractor with a forge, anvil and a hammer. He was good with the farm animals, both horses and with the cows. His creative independence in the workplace was an early inspiration for me. In truth I never saw him feel helpless in any farm situation.

Walter lived on the bottom floor of the farm house with his wife. The upper floor was taken up by Stephen and Irma. It was felt that there was no room in the farmhouse for us three boys when we were on the farm. Stephen had a Bunkhouse built for us right adjacent to the main house. It was one room, with a small heating stove and a bathroom no larger than the two necessary fixtures required. And the bathroom had no door. Life revolved around our meals with Walter and his wife, and doing work on the farm. Walter was also a good teacher. We learned the arts of milking machine, pitching hay, spreading pea vines in the silo, and many other things. There are only a few things to recall in more detail on the farm, because most of our time was spent in boarding school, Vancouver College.

On one occasion I contracted Whooping Cough. I recall sitting under a cherry tree for about three days, just coughing. During that time I only saw Irma once. She brought me a bowl of soup. In fact that was almost the only time I saw her that whole summer, although I saw Stephen every day.

One whole summer I also had a newspaper route. I had to pick up papers in "town" and deliver them over a lot of farm roads. Overall it was about 7 miles of bicycling every day. It was likely that this was the first money I earned myself. Not very much, but I was proud of it.

In the year when Peter Paul got his driver's license, Stephen got me a job at the local brewery. It was with a Hungarian friend of Stephen's, a Dr. Szėnyi, who was the brewery chemist. Whenever he had time, Peter would drive me to the brewery to work in the laboratory. I would run to get samples from Vats and do simple laboratory tasks. But to my regret I could not go there very often. The excuse was that gasoline was in wartime rationing, except for actual farm equipment. The tractor gas was supplied in 55 gallon drums, and could not be used for autos or trucks. I recall one day the fuel truck driver dropping off two of these drums on the farm. He opened each drum and then from an envelope like package he poured in a powder that turned the gasoline purple. The driver just carelessly tossed the empty powder packages on the ground. If police would stop a car and find it used purple gas, it meant serious jail time for the driver.

A little later, I picked up the packages, just to be neat. But I kept them and next time I was at the brewery laboratory I looked up the name of the powder in a book called the Merck Index. I read that the name was Alizarin Purple. It was a dye with special chelating characteristics for salts like calcium. On the farm we used lime, Calcium Chloride, as a ground sweetening fertilizer. So when I got back to the farm, I took a cupful of the purple gas, and added a teaspoonful of lime and mixed them together, to see what would happen. The purple color all went into the lime! I said Gee Whiz! And I showed it to Peter Paul. And he said Gee Whiz!

We made a deal. Perhaps it was the first deal for both of us. I would make enough colorless gas for the truck to support trips to the brewery and also for Peter Paul to go on dates. And he would drive me to the brewery. It was of mutual benefit. And that is how I first became interested in chemistry, like dyes. And that was my first piece of "productive" research.

During the school year we were boarders at Vancouver College. Except for Peter Paul, who spent his last year of high school at Ladner, and worked on the farm all that fall and winter. The College was definitely a strong part of our training and formation. But for sake of brevity, this will not be part of our joint story.

Mr. Smith

Eventually STEPHEN GAVE up farming. He had served more than the time that Canada had required of an immigrant to be on a farm or in the lumber industry. The money from the farm was invested in a furniture factory. All sorts of un-painted furniture. And Peter Paul was proud that he was hired as one of his salesmen, even while he was still at UBC. It was one of his first real jobs.

Then one evening Stephen picked us up in his Pontiac and drove us to a street opposite to the furniture factory. We watched while the whole plant went up in flames.

The farm had not been a great success, although it could have been much worse. Here was a disaster that Irma could use to grind him into conviction that he had always been, and always will be, a failure.

We sat there in silence and watched the flames.

At some point Peter Paul started to discuss some college business theory with Stephen like they had often done. He started;

"There is this business man, Mr. Smith, from Venezuela. He had come into some funds and was about to make some investments, but had a difficult time deciding what to do."

The discussion went on, and eventually Stephen, in his analytical way, came to the conclusion that Mr. Smith had to invest where he could provide his own person as added value. And that is where the discussion ended for the night.

But the next day, and the next week, while driving around, or at dinner or just sitting and talking, Mr. Smith became an important person. He more and more resembled an insurance beneficiary who needed to do something with his money. And the details went something like this.

Mr. Smith knew the credit business. He and his family had been in the credit business, even internationally. There must be a new, creative, approach for which a market is ripe. Credit is the most powerful way to amplify a small lump sum of money. What was actually created was Coronation Credit, a Vancouver company. Stephen Halom, President, Peter Paul Saunders Vice President. As best I could understand it, Coronation began by giving a new type of second mortgage. At that time a highly creative finance medium.

The reason why I remember this so clearly, so many years later, is that the conversation totally bored me. I knew nothing of the business world. The words were not English or even Hungarian! And the discussion never stopped. Well I was wrong. I should have been listening and learning. I certainly agree that modeling is a creative way to plan.

The subtlety with which Peter Paul introduced the subject, and carried it forward, went totally unrecognized. The gradual switch from a theory to a viable business entity also went unrecognized. The gradual growth of interest and the intensity with which it was pursued were where Stephen began to take ownership. As an "uninterested" observer, I could only marvel at the process and the result. Some years later, when there was a disagreement on the direction of Coronation Credit, it was obvious to me that both of them felt strong ownership. And I was not at all surprised.

To this day I do not know if Mr. Smith is a standard model in academic business courses. I have taken a few psychology courses and I have not met up with the likes of Mr. Smith. My opinion is that three things were created on the night of the furniture factory fire; a distraction from the fear of feeling of failure, an academic model and the germ of an enterprise that grew to impressive proportions, as Peter Paul will describe in the chapters to follow.

The model with which I am very familiar is "the fly on the wall". Many times I have heard someone say, "I wish I were a fly on the wall, just observing some extraordinary happening." I fit that description in the case of Mr. Smith.

Other Summers

WHEN STEPHEN SOLD the farm it created a concern of what we should do during the summers. Stephen chose to distance us form Irma as much as possible, and so he sent Frank and me to a YMCA summer camp. Peter Paul was old enough to work and he did so at the furniture factory, at first, and when he graduated from University he almost immediately went to work at the Canadian Pacific Railway.

I mention the summer Camp here for just a few reasons. First, it was definitely a different character builder than Vancouver College. Second it serves the observation that both Frank and I were being shielded from a less institutional and more realistic life style. And third, there are just a few anecdotes here that are relevant to the rest of the story.

We started as campers. In subsequent years became counselors, or group leaders, and in my last year there I worked on the staff as the one who would prepare other children for camping independence. It is not only boy scouts who teach how to make fires, cook a basic meal from materials that 8 to 10 year olds can carry in a pack sack. I taught them also how to put that pack sack together so that it would not fall apart on the trail. Then I would take the youngsters out overnight. I would sit on a fallen log in a completely isolated campsite, and say "OK boys,

I expect you to have dinner in half an hour, and your beds ready for the night." Amazingly there were no complaints, ever. And the dinners were usually palatable. And the lesson I learned is that expectation is a great motivator. I do not know where and when Peter Paul learned that lesson, but he used it all his business life, very successfully.

In this camp, there was one apparent, extraordinary, health hazard. It was a creek that entered Howe Sound, (the ocean) about 20 yards from the location of the senior camp sight, tents and storage places. Some 150 yards upstream the creek passed by the junior camp's latrines. There was an obvious drainage from one to the other. In between these two locations of the creek there was a trail and very small bridge crossing the creek. This was a dank and smelly place with very tall trees covering, and almost dark even in high daylight. It was a place that could not be avoided by senior campers as they went from the main camp to their more isolated area daily at least two or three times. I only mention it here because I shall talk more about it as I pick up my story after Peter Paul has completed his part.

The year that Frank and I were both counselors (leaders) at the camp, Frank grew a beard. I have to say that he was not yet ready to grow a beard. Anyway, the other leaders and staff publicized an ultimatum that the beard must come off or the leaders will jointly accomplish the same. The only ones against this idea were the tent group of campers who were Frank's charges that summer. The time came; it was an evening after all campers were in bed. A delegation of leaders came to Frank's tent. But the campers would not let them in. Eventually it was discovered that he was not even there, he was hiding somewhere else. The whole camp was in an uproar. No camper would be sleeping while this was going on. I have to admit that it was I who found him. He was at the top of the water tower, and I only knew because I saw a very small piece of fresh, wet dirt on the ladder leading to the top. Well the beard came off and there was peace thereafter. It was the only time that we brothers did not act in concert. And I still remember it with some mixed feelings.

However the main reason for describing the summer camp is

to explain that Frank, at this time had never been exposed to any living style except that of an institution. His fees for his personal maintenance had always been paid by Stephen up to this time. And when he went off to the seminary, that same lack of exposure to real life continued. He had never been in a position where he "earned his keep". Nor had he watched anyone else do the same. And that had a profound influence on his later life, as will become clear a bit later.

As for me, the summer after I was on Staff at Elphinstone and got paid for it, I started working at Lake Louise as a gardener. Peter Paul got me the position, and I must say that it was a most satisfying thing to be working and seeing a paycheck. Also I was totally on my own. I had to interact with a bunch of peers, mostly my age. And it was a lot of fun. I learned to mountain climb, and was actually helpful to the hired Swiss Guides. They would put me on the front end of a rope while crossing crevasses in the glaciers. I would cross an ice bridge because I was very light. The next in line was always the "fat lady". The guides would hold the rope on one side and I on the other, while she crossed. We never had an accident where she slipped down a crevasse. But I remember this as a wise precaution of the guides.

I did a lot of mountain climbing alone as well. This also is not advisable, but what a pleasure it was, after years of institutional close living, to be totally alone in a beautiful place of my own choosing! Please see the attached poem "Friends".

The second summer at Lake Louise was memorable for two reasons. One was that there was a new foreman in the gardens, who did not know his job. He was hired because he was a friend of the manager. There were two of us who had some knowledge of the gardens from previous years, and we were apparently a threat to this foreman. He sent us out one day to do an impossible job. It was to dig up a bed of Irises where the roots had been in place for many years. We failed, and he fired us both on the spot. However, I went straight to the manager, and said to him, "We both know that your friend did this to protect himself. There is no justification for it, and I expect you to fix it." The manager agreed! And he got me a job in the dining room as a bus boy.

Friends

At Lake Louise there is a trail
That leads one right around the lake.
I used to travel to its tail
And then away from it I'd break
And travel up the mountain side
On cougar tracks. Then I would hide
And watch the whole world open wide.

How strange, that cougars, hated by all men
Afford the trails I traveled then.

The valley down below, one time
When I was on a cougar's track
Sent out a beauty so sublime
It seemed to call and call me back.

But on I went on rocks so stiff.
Between two peaks, where Heaven ends.
I met a cougar on a cliff.
And we were friends.

She looked at me and nodded, so,
Not saying that I was her foe.
For equals being in that place
She merely looked upon my face.
And I, in turn looked in her eye.
She nodded then, and passed me by.

Summing up

HAVING READ THE foregoing, a polite reporter may ask,"How do you feel about your very eventful youth?"

To the hypothetical question I must give a rather long answer. And the answer includes some questions of my own.

But first, just a little more background.

In my very early years, when I was no more than three or so, our whole family was accustomed to go for walks in the neighborhood around our house. I was so small then that walking hand in hand with both my parents I would swing between them as they walked. I am sure that many of us have seen tiny youngsters do the same. On these walks we very often went past a crucifix right next to the side walk. I have since seen many of these all around Hungary. They are part of the culture, an expression that the country wished to be identified with the Catholic Church. Often there were vases of flowers on the ground around the base of the wooden structure. When I was swinging along between my parents, I would look over to where this icon was, and I had no idea of what it represented. There was a scantily dressed person looking up into the sky. (Heaven was not in my vocabulary.) What I am saying is that my parents had shielded me from all consideration of religion. It had just not been mentioned during those years. I very quickly add that maybe it was mentioned, and it just went right over my head.

I do have a memory of being baptized around my age of 6 in a very large church. But this too is an isolated incident and I am very certain that it had no meaning to me at the time. And there was a third incident in which a young teaching assistant at my first grade in school tried to explain to me the beginnings of a catechism. It had a picture in it of an old bearded man sitting on a cloud. Once again, if this meant anything more to me at the time it is long gone form my memory. In retrospect, those were the only three exposures I had to any form of religion until the time we three brothers arrived at St. Ignatius College, Riverview, Sidney.

Indeed our parents seemed to shield us from a variety of things in those early years. I do not remember ever being out in the rain. Not once was I wet when outside our house, except when we had gone skiing. Politics, race and money were the other subjects never discussed in at least my presence. If I now try to evaluate this shielding from possibly stressful subjects I find it very strange. Hungary, at this time was in the middle of political turmoil. From 50 years before the time of our father's birth in 1897 up till the end of the Second World War, Hungary went through a series of shattering changes. When the Austrian emperor pushed out the Turks from Hungary the Hungarian plains were suddenly very under populated. The void was filled relatively quickly by German speaking Austrians and by Jews who immigrated from a number of countries including Russia, and Poland. They joined an existing minority of previously present Jews. The native Hungarians, called Magyars, welcomed this population influx and there was a very fast process, called assimilation. All groups quickly spoke only Hungarian, and all began to blend into one culture. A spirit of nationalism became very strong. And around the turn of the century it took on the goal of independence from Austria. A startling statistic is that in 1900 only 51% of the Hungarian population was Magyars! And all the ethnic groups were well represented in parliament.

At about the same time, Hungarian history began to change.

Cities, especially Budapest, began to flourish. A group of professional people began to appear. Real estate as a business began to be important. The financial skills of the Jews came to be of great service to all of Hungary and they were encouraged to be involved. Then gradually the mood changed and resentments grew. Resentments disappeared because the government, even the prime minister, strongly defended this class of professionals. It was even said that they added qualities to the Hungarian culture that others should learn. Attitudes of religion, nationalism and liberality in government pulsed back and forth depending on the rhetorical skills of governmental figures and writers at any time.

Our grandparents and parents were right in the middle of this pulsing, changing environment. Our father was chief legal counsel to the Real Estate Bank of Hungary, and later the bank's CEO. From the books he wrote there is no doubt that he was one of the most knowledgeable experts on the subject of Credit and Credit law, when real estate was in a spiraling growth period. Uncle Leo was the president of a bank. A different bank. Our father knew the politics of the time clearly. And yet his attitudes were not passed on to his children.

As part of the answer to the hypothetical reporter's question I say that I now have some feeling that I was not just shielded from those realities but denied some potential for growth experience during my formative years. Would better knowledge of the times have changed me in those years, or was it all irrelevant since I never grew up in that environment? On the other hand, I was left with a skill that came on me very suddenly. That is the skill of a child accepting changes in surroundings and accepting that which I had no control to alter.

Now to my own questions.

Why did my mother take her own life? And why at just the time when she did? It may seem that as a nine year old, I may not have known my mother very well, and would be excused for not answering that question. And as nine year old I could not have done so. I barely even understood what happened. In a way, I was fortunate in acquiring a book that helped me in several ways. When Grandmother Margit came from Budapest in 1949 to Vancouver she brought with her a number of items that we could call family treasures. One of these was my mother's diary. Most diaries are written to be never read by others. Under the circumstances I believed that I was justified in learning more about my mother. I not only read it all, I eventually translated it form the original Hungarian as a gift to my brothers and to all our children.

Grandmother Margit had a saying, "When you negotiate with somebody, you must get into their heads." I believe this saying also deserves attention when trying to understand a person in a historical context. Indeed, history is the context in which I should try to answer my own questions.

Our mother was a very sensitive person. She writes in the diary at first as a typical teen-ager, on her observations about boys, about dance classes, about vacations in various countries, and about her love for her parents. She then also observes a beggar sitting outside her school and expands her concern to an untold number of people who are starving, while she also recognized that her family is living a life of wealth. She was greatly distressed at this but knew little of what she could do as a child. She accounts for how on a number of occasions she gave her school lunch to the beggar and had very mixed feelings about not being able to do more.

She also writes in her diary about her strong attachment to her family. To her mother and father, and to her brother, Stephen. She also writes about extended family, and includes description of a fight with her cousin Lilly. I also saw a page in the diary with a note from Lilly, on how much she loved my mother. And later another note that mother was over her fight and loved Lilly for her understanding friendship. The diary stops suddenly just a few months before her marriage, in 1926, with an unexplained note of fear of being discovered in her sadness. But there is no explanation of the cause. Maybe there is no cause, and this is the only witness of a developing depression.

Then there is the historic context of the nuptial agreement, with its dowry and the understanding that if there was a separation mother walked away with a sizable fortune. Children were not mentioned in that agreement. It may have been a failure of anticipation in light of developing events. That part may not have been customary in those days.

Thus I can piece together a mother who was sensitive, moody, strongly attached to family. She was likely strongly shielded form life beyond her home, school, dance classes, and religious practice. She was not accustomed to making decisions for herself, even after some 13 years of marriage. That is not totally unusual, even in present society.

The Future prospects in Hungary would have been very difficult for her to understand. Confusion between religion and ethnic origin was a very subtle argument, and neither the German Nazis not the Hungarian equivalent of the Arrow Cross cared to make that distinction in the middle of a racial attack. Our father would have had great difficulty in having her understand a reason for not returning home at the end of summer in 1939. Even the fact that Stephen and Irma passed through Zurich and left for a very far place is likely not to have registered, since her sense was that Irma should be as far from the rest of family as possible. The time was coming closer for all of us going to a very far place. She did indeed have a choice of separation and going back to Hungary. There was sufficient communal funds and property there so that she could have easily managed. Well, not so easily, because she had no business skills at all. She may not even have considered that option although she must have known the preparation our father made since our passports are full of visa permissions to enter a variety of countries we never actually visited, starting in July 1939. When the reality finally came to her it is understandable that a will to live waned away. She hid it well and I believed she even surprised our father. He was so focused on building a brand new future and was busily sorting opportunities. He was not entirely ignorant of her longings for home. I have in an ancient file from a business assistant of his Budapest carding brush factory a letter that responds to father's request to send some Hungarian sausage to Zurich because mother would have liked it.

For me the events at that time went so fast that I must have gone into a mode of acceptance. Mother was no longer with us. It was a defense reaction, I should imagine, and I cannot explain it.

If I am asked how I feel about it now, I must say that her action is understandable although not really acceptable. But I have long ago forgiven her for denying me her presence and continued love. Also I recognized that her absence has no doubt changed my life. But I cannot really tell how. It is a shame that she had not remembered the beautiful and inspiring story of Ruth form the Bible:

> *Wherever you go I shall go.*
> *Your people shall be my people*
> *And your God shall be my God.*

In the weeks and months that followed I did not have feelings of difficulty. I had great faith in our father, and if he made decisions for what was best for us all, I could only follow. Attending school became a source of stability and created a surrounding of reality. And I had no deep thoughts about a personal loss.

I do not have to ask the same question about our father's death. His letters to his three sons and to Mrs. Foster in Melbourne are very clear. His depression was uncontrolled and it had come on very suddenly. He had made so many plans for a future in Australia, and was looking towards a new life too much to have anyone believe that he had a long term plan to terminate his own life. He had overcome the most difficult of journeys with a burden of sorrow and a troop of youngsters and had in his possession a small fortune with which to carry forward. The loss of our mother must have come on him suddenly, when the calm after the stormy escape we had accomplished became a time to recollect. It overcame him. He could not help himself, and we children were not able to help. We were all strangers in a strange land. There was no one to talk to. Here there is nothing to forgive. Nor do I have any feelings of guilt for not having helped.

Instead, my memory of our father is one of a very brave man who made brilliant and very difficult decisions in a very difficult time. The eye witness stories of Eva and also of Tommy about what Budapest was like just a few months and a few years after our father took us away from that danger certainly validates fathers plan. Everything he did, while he was in control was well planned, well executed and absolutely correct.

I only want to add one comment. I never realized our father's appreciation of poetry. My own interest started much later. I only know of his interest because we have somehow preserved a small file in which he translated poems by Henry W. Longfellow into Hungarian. One of these poems may have been on our father's mind during those last days of his depression:

Jugurtha By HW Longfellow.
> *How cold are thy baths, Apollo!*
> *Cried the African Monarch, the splendid,*
> *As down to his death in the hollow*
> *Dark dungeon he descended,*
> *Uncrowned, unthroned, unattended.*
> *How cold are thy baths, Apollo!*
>
> *How cold are thy baths, Apollo!*
> *Cried the Poet, unknown, unbefreinded,*
> *As the vision, that lured him to follow,*
> *With the mist and the darkness had blended.*
> *And the dream of his life was ended.*
> *How cold are thy baths, Apollo!*

Jugurtha
> **Forditotta Szende Péter Pál**
>
> **Milyen hideg fürdöid Apollo!**
> **-Kiáltott fel a gazdag uralkodó-**
> **Amint leszállt a halál országábon,**
> **Románnak rideg, nyirkos fogságába,**
> **Ö kinek volt, de nincs koronája.**
> **Milyen hidegek fürdöid Apollo!**

Milyen hidegek fürdöid Apollo!
- Igy szólt a nem ismert, nem kegyelt iro,
Látomástól csábitva, hogy kövesse
Mindazt, mi sötét burokkal van fedve;
Igy vált élete álmának vége.
Milyen hidegek fürdöid Apollo!

I understand my reaction at the time as one of strong defenses built in the first tragedy that carried over to the second. I accepted the childhood that was given me and the fact that there were still people who could look after me. And the feelings of tragedy that could have overcome me were suppressed. This self defense has followed me over life to an extent that sometimes I have seemed to be a "cold", un-reactive, person who does not show much feeling. Perhaps that is so, and perhaps there is cause. Perhaps it has saved me from a lot of pain.

I grieve more for my parents now than I did anytime as a child.

The reality that followed, however, was what the hypothetical reporter calls an eventful childhood. Not just hypothetical, I have had good friends probe for my feelings of that time and later. Usually there came a question that probed too deep and I made an excuse not to continue. I know also that both Peter Paul and Frank went through the same reactions, even with our children. Hence I feel an obligation to respond now.

One aspect may have helped me was a degree of uncertainty. I was shielded from a confirmed knowledge until I was much older. Indeed confirmation about my father came when I was helping to deal with Peter Paul's personal papers some time after he passed away. That is when I found the letters that I translate in the Melbourne chapter, above. That clearly was not the case for Peter Paul. He was the one who shielded me. It must have been a burden for him to carry for so long. Perhaps he even forgot that I did not know.

All three of us were shielded from another, obvious, reality. During our childhood no one ever even hinted at, or spoke the word "orphan" in our presence. This was so at Stephen's home, at Vancouver College, at summer camp. We never had a label that may have put us at a disadvantage, a label that gave us an excuse to do less than to excel. It worked. At least for me there was never a feeling that I was different in any way except that my original language was not English.

I even accepted, a few years later that Irma was no substitute for a lost parent. More to the point I had great distress for Stephen that his wife was a difficult person as a lifelong partner. He did his best for all of us in spite of her resistance and self centered pity of her own loss of the good life. Even when Stephen was later able to supply Irma with a good life she did not change. One could say a lot more about this woman. But why bring up those times, and those feelings?

There is one good thing to say about Irma. She was an excellent cook. In her cooking she did her best to preserve the one part of the good life in Hungary over which she had some control. Both she and Stephen enjoyed the good Hungarian food. So did I on a few occasions.

As a result of all these circumstances, most, but not all, of our growing up happened at Vancouver College until each of us in turn graduated. On a few weekends we were "home" with Stephen on the farm. If he would drive us to church, for example, he would be asking questions about the sermon on the way home. He always needed a report of our activities at "the College". He did represent an adult figure on whom we could rely. He had wisdom in preventing our extended exposure to Irma. We never questioned his decision to put us in a boarding school. Hence we always looked forward to our time on the farm and did identify it as home. A home in a bunk-house, where three youngster were often together and formed a deep bond.

At the College, however, the three brothers had entirely separate lives. Separate friends, separate interests and we met mostly only at the dining hall. We were, however, under the charge of the same Irish Christian Brothers who were professionals at the mental, spiritual and physical growth of young boys. Indeed, in retrospect, their job became easier with us because there were very few outside influences. It was not like the day students, who went home every day. The Brothers had an advantage, also because there were many of them, rather than our having only one parental model. We could admire one for his logical thinking. That was Brother Stoehr. We could admire another for his organizational skills. That would be Brother Walsh, the principal. We could relate to a dedication to music, and a dedication the children in his charge. That was Brother Victor Castle.

There were a few items to which we objected. One was waking up early to go off to Mass at St. Peter and Paul, two blocks form the dormitories. The only good thing about that was that I learned not to shiver in the cold walk by sheer will power. If I wanted to I could not shiver. If I wanted, I could shut out my surroundings and not pay attention to a Latin ceremony that I already knew from memory. That enabled me to look forward to the new things to learn every day. Those new things were my life.

Unfortunately the other item to which I objected was the daily rosary in the chapel. The Brothers were excellent teachers, excellent disciplinarians, superb in providing moral support for young boys. How could they have understood that there was a second meaning to the oft repeated prayers that begins with "Our Father"?

As a result of my whooping cough I am left with a nervous scar somewhere that makes me very sensitive to throat irritations. I sometimes still have fits of coughing just like I did under the cherry tree. I also have some scars in my knees form the swings and flying into the sand box. I do not think I have any other scars from that period of my life. This is not exactly so for Peter Paul. He was old enough to remember our father much better than I. He came to an adult life with a very strong drive to be like father. He had a drive to succeed in business like our father, and to be like father in many other ways. Some of this was good. He developed social skills that I never mastered. Indeed his understanding of credit may have been inherited along with the books of Hungarian credit law that our father wrote. Hunting became part of his life. Golf even more so. Was the drive to excel at whatever he did in

PETER PAUL SAUNDERS

UNFINISHED MEMOIRS

1928 - 1981

As dictated to Trudy Lynne Weeks
April 2007 – June 2007

IN THE BEGINNING

I WAS BORN IN 1928, which was the last year of prosperity in the roaring 20's. In 1929, the market crashed and in 1930, the Depression started. I was the first son of Peter Paul and Elizabeth Szende. I was given my father's name, but in addition to that, they added John and George.

The Depression did not seem to have any affect on our family in Hungary. We lived in a big house with five acres of garden and the required number of servants.

My brother Frank was born in 1929 and in March of 1931, perhaps my earliest memory, is sitting in the garden with my father, listening to the news that another brother, Alexander, was born. The three of us were quite close in age so we always managed to play well together. We had one family of close friends who had two children, one my age and one Alex's age. Our nanny was always an Austrian girl who spoke no Hungarian and therefore we all became bilingual with German at a very early age.

Next door to our property, my grandmother, (on my mother's side), had a house which she and my grandfather only occupied in the summer. The two properties combined had about ten acres of garden complete with sandbox and orchards with fruit trees, so we had lots of room to play.

When I reached six years of age, I started school. I went to a private school, which in addition to the normal curriculum, taught English, and that is where I first received the grounding in the language that is now my first choice.

As I said, the Depression did not seem to affect our family, but there was considerable concern as to what was going on in Germany. A new Government was formed with a dictator heading it who's powerful ranting attracted considerable support in his Country. It became obvious that his policies of severe anti-Semitism were going to create considerable hardships and that his dream of conquering the World would not be easily contained. As time went on, it became more and more clear that Germany was arming for another major war. Austria was annexed, as were parts of Czechoslovakia and Poland was threatened. My father decided that since war was inevitable, he would like to take his family out of Europe and as he had business contacts in Australia, we were going to immigrate to that Country. My mother had passed away, so it was just my father, my brothers and I.

Once war had broken out, travel was restricted however we were booked on a ship out of Genoa, Italy which we missed. We then decided to go by air. Royal Dutch Airlines, KLM, had flights leaving Athens and ending up in Australia. The planes had limited range in fuel and other areas, so we were to stop every night and spend the night. The first night was in Alexandria, Egypt. There were also stops in Basra and Baghdad in Iraq; Jodhpur in India; Rangoon in Burma; and Batavia in the Dutch East Indies. We then changed planes to a smaller one and spent the next night on the Island of Bali. Eventually we landed in Darwin, the northern point of Australia, and henceforth flew to Brisbane and then Sydney.

In Sydney, we were enrolled in a very fine Jesuit school called St. Ignatius Riverview. The School had superb grounds. Three football fields, six handball courts, its own Infirmary, ferry dock in the harbour and an observatory run by a Father O'Connell, who years later I visited in Rome where he was the head of the Vatican's Observatory.

My father having passed away, the Australian Government was trying to decide what to do with three orphans. One choice was to ship us back to Hungary, where our grandparents lived. Another to Canada where an uncle, my mother's brother lived in Vancouver. Fortunately, the decision was made to go to Vancouver, and we had a choice of flying in October '41 or February '42. We elected to go in October, which turned out, to be a very good decision as after Pearl Harbour, in December 1941; all further passenger flights were cancelled.

Once again, the range of the planes was short and so the flight on the "Pan Am Clipper" stopped every night. Our flight originated in Auckland, New Zealand. The first night we stayed on a yacht in Numea, the next night, on the Equator in the Canton Islands where we had a chance to swim in the warm water of the Equator. Hence, we went to Honolulu, which in those days was quite undeveloped. I remember having a 20-course dinner at the Moana Hotel under the banyan trees. I was 13 years old and the eldest of the three, and so I had the responsibility of looking after my two brothers, which weighed quite heavily on me during this trip. The last leg was an overnight flight to Los Angeles and a hop up to San Francisco where Uncle Stephen met us and relieved me of the responsibility of being in charge. We traveled to Vancouver by train and on arrival met our Great Uncle, Leopold Horvath, who was the first member of our family to come to Vancouver in the 30's. We were enrolled in Vancouver College as borders and of course felt strange with our Australian accents for which the boys teased us. Fortunately, we lost them quickly. Hungarian immigrants to Canada in those days were encouraged to become farmers, and as such Uncle Stephen had bought a farm in Ladner. We would go out there on weekends, and over the years learned quite a lot about farming, and made some friends. We would spend the summers there and by the time, I was 15 I was participating in community farming activities like thrashing, where various farmers would get together with their horses and wagons and haul the grain to the thrashing machines to keep them running full time. I learned to load the wagons with bales of hay as well as the grain. No bale weighed less than 100 pounds and some as heavy as 125. I think some of the arthritis, which I developed in later years, might have been caused by heavy lifting in those days. My brothers and I were always close together and while Stephen would have liked to have been closer to us, his wife was not ready to take on three fairly active boys.

Peter Paul at five years old, and at 23.

Frank, Peter Paul and Alex 1949

Peter Paul At his desk at home.

Uncle Leo, Grandmother
and Peter Paul at Banff.

Peter Paul Szende (Hunting picture)

Peter Paul Saunders
(Hunting picture)

2

After graduating from Vancouver College, I went to the University of British Columbia where I was enrolled in the Commerce Faculty. I found the courses challenging as I was the youngest in my Class. Only sixteen years old at the time, and therefore I did not participate in any of the real social activities of the University. I always had one or two very good friends, but that was the extent of my social life.

When it came time for me to graduate I was 19 years old and I was part of the graduating class where the first group of veterans, some as old as 25 were also graduating. It was difficult to find a job, but I put my name down for BC Electric, which was the major utility in British Columbia. Forty people applied for the one job they had and without any criteria, they reduced the number to ten who would be interviewed. Fortunately, I was in the ten and after my first interview, I was still among the five who they were considering. I was given an aptitude test and eventually called in to the psychologist to discuss my results. I was disappointed to hear him say that while I did well in the test I would not be considered for the job in the accounting department. When I asked why, he showed me a graph and explained that I had very high abilities, but weaknesses when it came to detailed work. I was disappointed and decided that I could not be as bad as they said I was and then did manage to get a job in the accounting department of the Canadian Pacific Railway. I was there for three years, had numerous promotions, but I understood that accounting was not to be my future.

One day while I was still in university, I was given a ride in a car that stopped and picked up a hitchhiker (Andrew Saxton) who spoke very knowledgeably about Hungary. When we were dropped off I started to speak to him and found out that he had recently arrived from Hungary and that we had quite a lot in common. We became very good friends.

While I was in accounting with CPR, I started to think of what I might do to change my vocation. I found that there were companies formed by young men of my age with small investments, dabbling in a variety of activities. I spoke to my friend Andrew Saxton about this and we decided that we would try to put together some kind of an investment company of this type.

Just after I graduated, my grandmother arrived from Hungary intending to stay a year and visit with her grandchildren, her son, her brother, and us. She thought she would furnish an apartment for a year and so was followed by a whole railroad car full of furniture, paintings, silver, china, crystal and other necessities. She did not realize how small the apartments were in Canada compared to what she had in Budapest, and in the end she could not use all the things she brought and thus distributed the contents to other members of the family. She was 65 years old and had never cooked a meal in her life, but decided that since she was set up in apartment she had better learn to cook and became quite successful at it. As time went on, she had me to dinner many times which eventually turned in to pretty much every night. In addition to the food, she distributed a lot of wisdom, including such statements as; "giving to charity has never made me any poorer; water finds its own level; when you negotiate, think with the other person's head"; along with many others. After awhile I asked her if Andrew could be included in the dinners and he became more or less a member of the family.

In the early 50's grandmother and Uncle Leo, her brother, and I would holiday together at Jasper Park and Banff. We were at the Jasper Park Lodge the night it burnt down and as we were staying in a cottage, we could stay the night, but had to leave the next day. Luckily, we were able to get rooms in the Banff Springs Hotel and so we drove the two hours between the two resorts. We spent several summers at Banff where I would play 36 holes of golf in a day, 18 in the morning and 18 in the afternoon. One year I joined up with a Texan who was a few years older than I and who wanted to play for big money, which I could not afford. Fortunately, I played well enough that I never lost and so we had a good time.

3

WHEN ANDREW AND I decided to form an investment company, we started to talk to our friends in order to put together the capital needed for this venture. One by one subscribers were found for amounts in the 100's of dollars. We found that if we were using capital to make loans with security such as automobiles, then the Bank would lend us four dollars for every one we put in ourselves, so that constituted the makings of a business, for which we needed a name. One day, one of our shareholders, Hall Brodie, was looking out the window of his office, saw an Imperial Oil truck, and came up with the idea that the Company should be called Imperial Investments.

In getting the business off the ground, we had two problems. We had to find customers for the loans, but before that, we had to raise the capital that would eventually be matched by the Banks. One of our fellow shareholders worked as a bellhop at the Hotel Lake Louise. One day while he was carrying up the bags for an American from Los Angeles they started chatting and he found out that the American was looking for Canadian investments. He put him in touch with me and he ended up being one of our largest shareholders at the time for a sum of $10,000.00. Over the years, Paul Kirby, this gentlemen, and our family became good friends. He was the producer of "Rosalinda" a musical that ran on Broadway for two years.

Our office was in the Standard Building, a desk in our lawyer's office. During my coffee breaks at the CPR, I would run across to what was the Eaton's store, rush to the Standard Building, read the mail, answer the phones and administered the business. At this time, I found that my last name was a disadvantage in being difficult to spell, hard to pronounce and generally time consuming. I therefore decided to change "Szende" to "Saunders". It took a little while to get accustomed to the new name, but it turned out to have been a good decision and over the years saved me a lot of time and trouble.

As the business grew, it became more difficult to administer in the way I just described and it looked like it could afford to hire me on a full time basis with a modest salary.

Shortly after I gave my notice at the CPR, the Government brought in credit restrictions, so the borrowings for our business became virtually impossible. We had a sympathetic bank manager though who helped us as much as he could, but we had to learn to live with the new restrictions, which luckily did not last too long.

As we grew and became more successful, it became easier to raise more money and we started to look for sources of loans such as automobile dealers. We managed to sign up a number of these and by this time, Andrew joined me, and became the second employee of Imperial Investments.

One of our friends, an accountant, decided to spend part time in our office, so he did our books and eventually we could even afford a secretary. As things progressed, we opened our first branch in Vernon, British Columbia with a manager who used to work for one of our competitors and who being local there, had the connections to attract business.

During this time, my brother, Alexander, had been attending Stanford University in California. He got his undergraduate degree, met the love of his life, and they were married in May of 1955. His best man and I drove down to the wedding, which we did on a non-stop basis so that we could afford to take a detour to Reno and participate in one of the shows. One of the attractions was a hypnotist who gave you the equivalent of eight hours sleep in ten minutes, and so since neither of us had slept on the way down, we wanted to take advantage of this offer. Unfortunately, for some reason, it did not work, so we carried on to the wedding. Afterward, my grandmother who had come on her own, and my brother, Frank who was studying for the Priesthood in Ottawa, and I spent several days visiting different sights in the San Francisco neighborhood.

4

When I came back to Vancouver, I found that we were in the process of opening an office in Winnipeg, having opened one in Edmonton a few months before. I had an early morning, 8 o'clock flight, which I wondered if I would be able to keep my eyes open on the four-hour trip. By coincidence, I was guided to a seat next to a very nice young lady who being a nurse, greeted me with a very cheerful "good morning". We had the most interesting conversation about a variety of things. Her name was Nancy McDonald from New Westminster and she was on her way to Toronto to graduate from nursing which she had taken at the Toronto General Hospital.

She was very knowledgeable about business affairs, various institutions in the Country and told me that she and her parents were going to visit in Europe after her graduation. Since I had not been back to Europe, I asked her to write me with her impressions when she returned to Canada. I really enjoyed meeting her and was hoping that I would hear from her again.

The Winnipeg office opened and after some minor problems, it got off to a good start. By now, we had offices in Vancouver,

Vernon, Edmonton and Winnipeg and were becoming a small factor in the finance business in Canada.

In September, I received a letter from Nancy telling me about her experiences in Europe and what her plans were in Toronto. I was on my way to a convention in Chicago and had planned to go on to Toronto to open an office there, so I telephoned her and suggested that we meet for dinner after I got to Toronto. I was going to have some of my friends who had attended the convention with me so I asked her if she could bring a couple of girls so that we could have a party. On the appointed day, Nancy and two of her friends came to the hotel and the six of us had a very pleasant evening until quite late at night. As I was going to stay in Toronto for a week to get the Branch going, I arranged with Nancy that we would meet for dinner the next day. Luckily, for me she was familiar with a number of good eating-places in Toronto, including one which turned out to be a Hungarian restaurant. We dined together every night for a week and I became less anxious to finish my work in Toronto and ended up staying for another week. We had seen a lot of each other and got along very well, so one evening while we were dining in the Royal York Hotel, I popped the question and we became engaged.

Shortly afterwards I returned to Vancouver and was told to present myself to her parents in New Westminster, who were not only shocked that she became engaged to somebody no one knew and in such a short time, but to make things worse, a Hungarian with an uncertain future in a business that they did not understand and a different religious background.

I went to see Mr. and Mrs. McDonald and was looking forward to meeting them not quite aware of the hang-ups that they had about me. Mr. McDonald had been a partner and manager in one of the larger forestry companies in BC, which had been bought out by the second largest a few years earlier. He was well versed in industry but was not a financier.

I took them a present as a souvenir, a small silver tray that Grandmother had brought from Hungary and tried to present myself in the best possible light. In hindsight, I would measure my success as being limited, however, since we were engaged and Nancy did return to New Westminster, subsequently, I saw a lot of her and of her parents.

After Christmas, a number of us went to Banff for a skiing holiday. Banff was very lively around that time and we enjoyed ourselves with good skiing and many parties in the evenings. When we returned we set a date for our wedding in February and before that various members of her family and friends entertained us.

Her first idea was that we should spend our honeymoon in a trailer; however, I persuaded her that a trip to Europe might be more interesting. One of the people working for me had worked for a financial business in England and had good connections with automobile dealers. He arranged for me to buy a Jaguar at more or less wholesale price, which we would pick up in England and would become my wedding present to Nancy. We were married in February and being a mixed marriage the wedding was held in Christ Church Cathedral's chapel. Afterwards there was a reception at the Georgian Club, a very fine establishment and a top ladies' club in Vancouver. My mother-in-law persuaded her husband that in spite of his being a teetotaller, champagne had to be served. I was too busy with all the guests and the preparation of my reply to the Toast to the Bride to take advantage of this, but it was an enjoyable and successful reception.

5

IMPERIAL INVESTMENTS' REQUIREMENTS for capital had grown to the point where we had investment dealers as underwriters. One of them found out that Laurentide Acceptance Corporation, a Quebec company about half as big as we were might be for sale and used very strong persuasion to get me to launch our European trip out of Montreal. The first stop of our Honeymoon was in New York, where we spent a couple of pleasant days and hence went on to Montreal. I received a phone call in our suite in the Windsor Hotel from an old Vancouver friend, John Rook, who it turned out, was living in Montreal. He was chosen to become General Manager of Power Corporation, a company started by the principals of Nesbitt Thomson, investment dealers. Power Corp. controlled almost every utility in Canada from BC Electric to Nova Scotia Power and had other investments in the forestry and petroleum sectors. This was a great responsibility for John at the age of 30, but he was very interested in what I was doing and thought that our Industry might be one that Power Corp. should participate in. Eventually, after several meetings, they did purchase enough voting shares to take control of our Company, but gave long-term management contracts to both Andrew and myself.

My meeting with Leopold Renaud, Chairman of Societe d'Entresprise du Canada, a holding company that controlled Laurentide Acceptance took place on a very friendly basis. He asked me to investment some money in his Company and become one of his Directors.

After a few days in Montreal, we flew to London, England. This was an overnight flight on a Stratocruiser, which had a very attractive bar on the lower deck and part of the upper deck with bunks, included a double one, which we were able to obtain. In London, we stayed at the Dorchester Hotel, a fine establishment with such surprising conveniences as heated towels in the bathroom. There was a lot for us to see in London and the few days we spent there went by very fast. Finally, we hired a driver to pick up Nancy's new Jaguar and drive us out to the Kent countryside, as we did not want to take a chance on the London traffic with our new car. I took over the driving on the highway and we went to a small airport where we boarded a plane and flew the car and ourselves over to Calais in France. We started our drive to Paris and found that as noon approached, we were getting hungry. We found a cozy looking Inn where we were seated and suddenly realized that we now had to speak French. I knew very little. Nancy had taken it in school, so she had a vocabulary, but her pronunciation was not understood. I thought menus all over the world were written in French, so we asked for a menu. Nancy, not to be out done, asked for two menus. The owner left us, walked to the bar and brought us two nice glasses of sherry, which we thought, was a nice French custom, but we did not receive menus. Our friends in Paris told us that the proprietors, hearing Nancy say; "duex menu" misunderstood and thought we wanted dubonet. Eventually we did manage to get two ham sandwiches, which luckily he understood.

In Paris, we had reservations in the Claridge Hotel on the Champs Elysees. With our lack of French knowledge, it was difficult to get the right directions, but by following a police officer's directional point on a number of occasions, we finally found the Hotel. Both the sight seeing during the day and the nightlife in Paris were experiences, which we treasured, but it was starting to get cold as the heating system in the hotel was not very good, so we left and drove to Basel, Switzerland and the next day on to Zurich.

We stayed in the Baur au Lac Hotel near the lake, a very fine and luxurious establishment. There were various dining rooms that served great food and their bar had good entertainment, including a girl who sang in Hungarian one night. My great aunt and godmother, Tücsok, in Budapest, told us to look up a very old family friend of her's, Dr. Duft. He had been the President of Switzerland the previous year. He and his wife had us to dinner at their home which proved to be a very interesting evening. The next day when I came back to the hotel room, Nancy told me, somewhat surprised, that Dr. Duft had answered his phone in English when she had phoned to thank him for the evening. I asked her what he had said and it turned out to be "hello".

From Zurich, we made a number of interesting side trips in to the mountainside and saw quite a bit of Switzerland by car. Our next stop was in St. Moritz where we stayed at the Badrutt's Palace Hotel, owned by the same family for several generations. The hotel had a great international clientele English, American, German, Italian and many others. When Nancy decided to go to get her hair done, I borrowed mitts from the bellhop, rented boots and skis and decided to go to the top of the mountain and ski the famous St. Moritz ski hills. With my borrowed outfit and grey flannels, I was the worst dressed skier on the mountain, but nevertheless enjoyed the run.

When it came time for us to leave, our car would not start. We found out that the gas had frozen in the tank, but were fortunate that the Jaguar had two gas tanks and that the one on the sunny side was okay. We then drove through the tunnel to Italy and stopped in Milan for a few days. There were many interesting sights, including the famous mural of the Last Supper by Leonardo, a huge arcade full of shops and the Opera House, all within walking distance of our hotel. We went to the Opera one night and being Nancy's first experience at an Opera, it was fortunate to have La Traviata performed and La Scala, a musical bonus that we did not anticipate.

A few days later, we left and drove to Genoa where we admired the cathedral that was painted in black and white stripes like a zebra. We spent that night at San Remo on the Italian Riviera in a hotel in which we found, the next morning, that most of the guests had to have good memories to remember when they were 70 years old. As a honeymoon couple, we were a little bit conspicuous and left the next day for Monte Carlo. We spent an evening in a casino, but neither made nor lost a lot of money. From there we drove back to Paris and stayed at Claridge's for a couple of nights.

I received a phone call from Vancouver telling me that the new credit restrictions were legislated and that I had better plan on getting home as soon as possible. We were planning to visit Nancy's oldest friend who had married a Belgian and was living in Bruges, so the next day we intended to go there until the elevator at Claridge's became stuck between the main floor and the second floor. It was lunchtime and we had difficulty rousing anybody to help, but eventually they brought a ladder and since it was an open cage elevator, we managed to scramble down. We did get to Bruges later that afternoon, and Robert Weghsteen met us at our hotel. We had dinner at his parent's home in the beautiful countryside, spent the next day looking at art galleries, headed back to London and eventually to Vancouver.

When I got to the office the next day, there was a serious problem because of the credit restrictions. In order to meet our commitments, we had to cover a shortfall, which was done by passing the hat around between shareholders and relatives. Uncle Stephen commented that he did not think there was a big enough hat to collect all the money we needed. Once again, we survived this problem and after credit restrictions eased, we could carry on in a normal manner.

Leopold Renaud called a Board meeting, which I attended in Montreal. It turned out he was having some difficulties with the head of Laurentide Acceptance and since I was knowledgeable about the Industry, I had to try to point things in the right direction. As it was not going to work too well, he turned to me and said, why don't you buy our controlling interest, which I was very anxious to do, but needed additional capital to conclude. Fortunately, I could persuade Power Corp. to assist with some funding and so we concluded what to us at that time, was a very large and major acquisition. Roland Therien, who was President of Laurentide Acceptance, was not aware of this transaction and we met for lunch in his Club. He was quite shocked to find out that we now controlled his Company. After the initial shock, we became good associates. He was left to run the business in Quebec and we had a good operating relationship. This transaction did make us a truly National company and a much stronger competitor in the Industry, with enhanced growth potential. It also made a good impression in British Columbia for one of its companies to be taking over a substantial eastern business.

6

WHEN NANCY AND I returned from our Honeymoon, we stayed a week or so with her parents and then found a house to rent in the British Properties, where the owners had left for Europe for three months. We enjoyed our stay in that house and found that we had many friends in the general area, including the Saxton's who lived about five hundred yards from where we were. While I was working during the day, Nancy had a real estate agent show her homes, as we were looking to buy something when our lease period was over. We were pretty sure we wanted to stay in the West Vancouver area; however, after looking at numerous homes, we did not find anything suitable. Eventually we did find a house on University Hill which had a magnificent view and garden, and three rooms which were all thirty feet long or more. As the furniture, which we had out of grandmother's railcar, was all very large, we needed to find something that had the rooms and capacity to take it.

These large rooms were also helpful when we had a Company manager's meeting in Vancouver one year and we had hired two buses to bring managers and their wives to our house for a party. It was a little disconcerting since they all arrived at once. We did not know the wives and even I had trouble recognizing a number of the managers, but the reception was a success and the spirit in the Company, most of the managers being young, was very healthy and vigorous.

One winter we decided to take a trip to Nassau where one of Nancy's cousins was married to the Prime Minister, Sir Roland Symonette. We wrote them when we were coming and what hotel we were staying at and found when we got to the airport that there was a car and driver to meet us. He took us to the hotel, helped to carry up the luggage and was very happy to tell us that his last name was "Saunders" too. I knew that we were not related, quite apart from the fact that he was a black Bahamian. He told us to get ready, as he was then to take us to a party, an event of course, that we were not aware of. Unfortunately, during our stay in Nassau, Nancy had a miscarriage after which Margaret, her cousin, insisted that we should stay in her guest cottage. We spent a couple of weeks with them and got to know both Margaret and Sir Roland as good friends.

Sir Roland mentioned that they had problems in finding a source of mortgage money for many of the Bahamians. I felt that we could probably establish an office in Nassau and since we were in the consumer finance business, we could help to overcome this challenge. Together, we formed the Commonwealth Bank of the Bahamas. Imperial Investments owned 71% and Sir Roland 29%. Fortunately for us, among our Canadian employees a manager originally came from the Bahamas and had been born there. I persuaded him to return and become manager of the Commonwealth Bank. This turned out to be a very fortunate move since he knew his way around, the mentality of the people, and where customers lived, as most streets did not even have addresses. When the Bank opened there was great jubilation that the Commonwealth Bank was giving money away, however, a month later the shock settled in that the money also had to be paid back over a period of time. The Commonwealth Bank still exists in Nassau. Is a very successful and prosperous undertaking, and is basically still controlled by the Symonette family.

In Canada, the integration of Laurentide and Imperial had a

number of problems, a lot having to do with the relationship between managements in Vancouver and Montreal. While Montreal was a self-contained management, it did have to comply with Company policy and it took some time to have this function smoothly. We also arranged for me and the top executives in Vancouver to take French lessons, which were of some modest help, but did not enable us to function in Quebec.

The relationship with Power Corp. also produced some challenges, as they observed that at our meetings, both Andrew and I showed a mind of our own. John Rook explained to his seniors that you can not expect people who are strong and aggressive in building their own business to suddenly behave in a meek manner in meetings with large shareholders.

By 1960, the Company had grown substantially and was truly a National presence in Canada.

The requirement for funding continued and so we met investment dealers in New York who agreed to float, for us, what was a substantial issue of debentures. Borrowings in Canada were on a fully secured basis whereby each individual receivable was assigned to a Trust company who would then see that there was sufficient collateral behind the secured debentures. The American system operated differently, without security, with negative covenants instead. Therefore, our secured issue was going to be unusual in the New York market. We had a team of lawyers from the well-known firm of Dewey Ballantyne of New York in Vancouver putting together the financing for this issue. After working on it for more than a week, they approached me with some bad news. In the United Stated there is a Mortgage Broker's Act which deals with secured lending and it also defines if the security behind the debenture changes by more than a fixed percentage, then new appraisals must be made and a new issue to replace the old one. Since the security behind our Trust changed on a daily basis with new loans being placed and payments being applied, we would not be able to operate on a secured basis in the United States, but our Canadian commitments required all of our activity to be under the secured Trustee so there was an impasse, which created a big problem. I thought about it for a while and suggested that it might be possible to have the Canadian Trustee issue a Note in the required face amount and deposit that Note as security for the debenture. According to the lawyers, this was a suitable alternative, a rather simple solution to an almost unsolvable problem. The Debenture was issued and sold and we were the first Canadian finance company to borrow in the United States.

7

Around that time, we became aware that a company located in San Francisco, called Mercantile Acceptance was doing a similar business to ours, and was going to be sold by the widow of the controlling shareholder. We immediately approached them, but found that there were a number of other potential buyers involved. Mercantile was a very well run operation with branches all over California and the west coast of North America. A lawyer, Executor of the Estate, by the name of Chalmers Graham was handling the sale. We had numerous meetings with him and management and after a lot of effort convinced them that we were the best buyer of the company. We had Mr. Graham join the Imperial Board so that we had some continuity to the American operation and Andrew and I took turns visiting San Francisco on a regular basis, at least every two weeks. Once more, this acquisition materially increased our size and added substantially to our profitability.

Along the way, we had acquired a nice cottage at Crescent Beach, one-half hour drive from Vancouver, where Nancy's parents had a cottage and where she had spent her summers as a child. The husband of one of Nancy's cousins talked to me one day about a television station, which he and a friend were going to apply to the Canadian Government to operate in Vancouver. Their only problem was that they needed to show $1,000,000 worth of subscriptions for the shares and he wondered if I could help put it together. I talked to a number of my friends and found that there was sufficient interest to provide the additional capital required. There were hearings and various applicants for the TV License. Altogether five different groups, representing some of the wealthiest and most senior business people in Vancouver, as well as radio broadcasters who wanted to get into television. Art Jones who had a movie and photography business headed our group. He put together our Brief and made the presentation to the Government Board. It must have been a very difficult decision to choose a winner; however, in January 1960 we were informed that our group was chosen to hold the License. That had to be the second best news for me that week as our first daughter, Christine, was born at the same time. We were originally told that the capital subscribed would probably not be required as the License was in fact a "license to print money", according to Lord Thompson. To our surprise and disappointment, all of the money was required.

The antenna for the station was authorized to be placed on Burnaby Mountain. The Mayor of this suburb of Vancouver insisted that the office and studios should also be in Burnaby, in fact, he had chosen a site, which was definitely unsuitable. After awhile a location was found in a Web & Knapp development called Lake City, however, it became very difficult to negotiate a proper price for the land. By coincidence, our Company was doing some financing for Web & Knapp in eastern Canada and when they became aware of this problem, it was quickly resolved. A studio was built and the station went on the air, Halloween 1960.

It was losing money as the profitability was based on advertising and our management did not have a good handle on cost controls. One of our Directors asked at a meeting that if we were fully sold out at our rate card, how much money would we be making, to which the answer was, that we would only be losing something like 15%

on our capital. While our President did a wonderful job in getting the License, he was obviously not qualified to operate the station, so major cuts in the executive ranks was implemented, a very painful experience, but nevertheless necessary as henceforth, the station became modestly and eventually very profitable.

In the early 1960's there was a World's Fair in Seattle. We had several rooms in a motel for visiting dignitaries, which was appreciated, by many of our connections. The Symonette family decided that they would visit Vancouver and then go to Seattle on a family holiday. Bahamians, around that time, did not believe in staying in hotels, so they were going to come and stay with us at our house on University Hill. This created a problem as we had a master bedroom and two other bedrooms, one of which was occupied by our two-year-old daughter, Christine. We had to move her crib into the master bedroom so that Margaret and Sir Roland and their two sons would have sleeping accommodations at our house. I had recently acquired a barbecue and Sir Roland, being an expert, helped me to put it to good use. Christine was thrilled to have cousins arrive, but the boys being five and seven years old, completely ignored her. After a few days of a very pleasant visit, the "hotel owner" was impressed that she in fact had an English Lord staying with her.

8

My grandmother who had suffered a stroke and could only say one word, could show that she really liked Nancy, and subsequently was thrilled to see a great grandchild after Christine was born. You could tell by her tone of voice, the one word she was able to say, what her mood was, but it was unfortunate that having been a great communicator, she was no longer able to converse with us.

One afternoon at Crescent Beach, I read an article in the paper about a company in Montreal called, B.J. Coglin Company. It was started in 1860, Incorporated in 1870, the President was a chartered accountant and it had a very impressive Board of Directors. The share price in the market was $15.00 and it paid a $1.00 a share dividend, which was a very good return at 6%. I thought a company that old, with a CA as President would be conservatively run and likely have some hidden assets not appearing on the Balance Sheet. Therefore, we decided to make a major investment of 10,000 shares, which probably made us one of the biggest investors in the Company. Its main business was manufacturing rail car springs, but it had a subsidiary called "Watson Jack" which dealt in new and used heavy equipment. A few months after we made the investment they stopped paying dividends and it turned out that the inventory of used equipment was heavily over priced. The bank forced a major write down and had it not been for the "blue ribbon" Board of Directors, they would have called the loan. Naturally, I was upset and on my next trip to Montreal, I visited with the President who as it turned out was a CA by training only, and was actually a retired army colonel. I expressed my disappointment and asked what solutions they had in mind. One was they asked me to join their Board. The other was, to bring one of their managers from Ottawa, a UBC graduate who I vaguely knew, to Montreal to run the Company. Ron Chorlton took over, changed the Company's name to Wajax, cleaned out the obsolete inventory, established firm ground rules on trade ins and write offs, disposed of the spring business, and to make a long story short, turned the Company around. I served on that Board for 40 years until the mandatory retirement age. It turned out to be a very successful Company with numerous stock splits, dividend increases, acquisitions, expansions and difficulties that were settled mostly on the upside. I am one of their two Honorary Directors.

On that particular trip, I went to Ottawa after Montreal and had a date with Gowan Guest who was then Executive Assistant to Prime Minister Diefenbaker. Gowan and I closed the Chateau Laurier's bar that night, but before we did, he told me he had made an appointment for me to see the Prime Minister at 10 o'clock the next morning. He said Diefenbaker was very concerned about unemployment, which had risen from 2% to 4%, and he was going to ask me if I had any suggestions of what he could do about it.

I was awake most of the night thinking of what I might be able to recommend and sure enough when I saw the Prime Minister he did not waste any time, but brought up the unemployment problem. Having given it a lot of thought, I suggested that he might eliminate unemployment insurance and replace it with a larger payment to those who were taking steps to improve their education and abilities. Such as an unemployed electrician might study electrical engineering and so forth. His reaction was that it was a good idea, but politically unacceptable. Incidentally, a few years later a Liberal Government brought in the second part of my recommendation, that is it encouraged payment for better education and self-improvement, without the elimination of UIC.

Imperial Investments was operating very successfully; however it seemed to become a problem to have so many names under which we operated. Some of our customers moved around the country and did not know there was an office where they could make payments. The odd customer who became delinquent became difficult to follow up on. I wrestled with this problem and one night when I was thinking about it in Chicago, I realized that if we were to unify everything under one name, the problem could be solved. However, the Imperial name would have been an anathema in Quebec, and I was not sure how successful it would be in the United States. The solution, which emerged, was to change everything's name to Laurentide, but this was a bitter decision for me to make and I was sure that others' reaction would be similar. When I came home and told Nancy, she was shocked and other than threatening to divorce me, expressed thorough disappointment. The next day I called our Public Relations advisor who had done an outstanding job for us in a number of ways. His reaction was equally bad. Finally, when I explained to him the reasoning behind it, he agreed that he would do what he could to implement this decision. It took awhile to implement it, but eventually Laurentide Financial Corporation became a well-accepted fact in Canada and the other countries where we had operations.

9

THE TELEVISION STATION was having problems because the signal from Burnaby Mountain did not reach all of Vancouver and missed quite a large segment of the population. Around this time, Frank Griffiths, an old YPO friend, bought the television station in Victoria. He was one of the applicants for the Vancouver License and was disappointed when we got it. He owned CKNW radio station, which was the most listened to station in this area, and now got into TV through Victoria. He suggested that we merge the two companies and that we could also take advantage of Victoria's tower on Saturna Island. After lengthy deliberations, we decided to proceed that way and he now became a large shareholder in Vantel Broadcasting. Eventually he made an offer to buy all the TV shares from the shareholders for shares in his Company, Western Broadcasting. There were numerous potential buyers, all offering attractive prices, but we decided to accept his offer and since I now ended up with a lot of Western Broadcasting shares, and had known Frank for a long time, I joined his Board. Eventually Western Broadcasting expanded; buying stations in Calgary, Winnipeg,

Hamilton and smaller centers, and became an important factor in the Broadcast Industry in Canada.

By this time, we decided that we would like to move from University Hill to South West Marine Drive. A house became available and we bought it, recognizing that certain alterations would have to be done. A friend of mine, David Stern from Los Angeles, who had just done something similar, asked me if I realized what kind of expense I had undertaken. I said I felt comfortable as I had a written estimate, to which he replied; "your final cost will be double, plus 10%". Unfortunately, he turned out to be right.

Nancy unfortunately had several miscarriages and so we decided to adopt a child, partly because Nancy felt her life as an only child would have been much better if she had had a sibling. To our good fortune a baby girl was born at the time she was in the hospital with her last miscarriage. The Children's Aid Society, who had our adoption request for some time, thought she would be a good fit with us. So our daughter, Paula, came to our home at the same time as Nancy came home from the hospital, and she has been a pride and joy to the family every since. The new house had seven bedrooms so each child had a bedroom of her own and attached to Paula's bedroom, there was a bedroom for a nanny. Christine was very excited about her new sister, but disappointed that she was not ready to play with her right away. Over the years, this problem was solved.

Most things were very nice in the new house on Marine Drive, but we were disappointed in the fireplace mantle in the living room that was basically "a piece of furniture out of the kitchen". On one of my trips to Montreal, I wandered in to an antique store and asked them if they had any fireplace mantles. They had a number of them, but all taken apart in the basement of the shop. It was hard to visualize what they would look like, but I found one that I thought would do, had it shipped to Vancouver, installed in the house, and it turned out to be a great addition to the living room.

Shortly after we started to finance automobile dealers, it became apparent that it would be an advantage to have insurance available to our customers. We formed an insurance agency, called Coronation Insurance, and appointed Uncle Stephen to be part owner and manager. We also found that many of the car dealers required so called "capital loans" to improve their facilities. They expected the finance companies to provide these at low bank type interest rates, which were obviously unprofitable. Therefore, we also formed a mortgage company called Coronation Mortgage, which would be more generous with the amounts of capital loans, but charge the appropriate rate of interest, materially more than the Bank rate. Once again, Uncle Stephen was a partner and manager of this business which was operated in close connection with the insurance agency. This combination worked very well, was well received by the car dealers, and started to grow quite nicely on its own. After operating for several years, Uncle Stephen decided that he would like to run for Alderman in the City of Vancouver. This attracted a lot of publicity and I tried very hard to discourage him, as I did not feel that politics and the mortgage business would mix too well! I had no success in persuading him of this and so one afternoon he asked me to drop by his house and made a proposition that at a fixed price we would either buy him out or sell our shares to him. The Saxtons and we were planning a holiday in the Okanagan that weekend and Andrew and I discussed this proposition at the time. We concluded that we would be able to borrow the money to buy him out and it would be a good business decision to do that. Uncle Stephen was disappointed in this decision, but we acquired his shares, appointed a new manager, found some other investors and created a Board of Directors, and Coronation continued to grow at a very impressive rate.

Over the years, the new manager and his expansion plan started to offer consumer credit type of mortgages. This was in conflict with what Imperial Investments was doing and Andrew and I sold our shares to Bill Ferguson, one of the Directors, and severed our relationship with the Company.

10

Imperial's relationship with its bankers was very solid thanks to the borrowing formula, which was established and continued from the early days. The Bank Act, which was revised every ten years, was up for revision in 1956. Prior to this revision, the maximum interest that a bank could charge was 6%, but the revision in 1956 removed this ceiling. Over the next few years, not only did the banks start to increase the rates they were charging on a variety of loans, but also began to look around for new areas that they might like to get in to, including the consumer finance business. Thus, by the early 1960s, the wholesalers of our money were starting to become our competitors, a situation, which was dangerous and detrimental to our business. Accordingly, I recommended to our Board of Directors that we should form a Bank of our own. We had been positioning ourselves in this direction by placing our Canadian branches at street level and in shopping malls to give them the appearance where they looked like banks.

The procedure to form a bank required a Charter from Parliament to be passed by both the Senate and the House of Commons. We found Senator Cameron from Banff, Alberta willing to sponsor this

Bill and so the first steps were taken to form the Laurentide Bank. The existing Chartered banks took a very negative attitude to this and started to pressure some of our Directors to cancel this program. The Laurentide Board decided that it did not wish to continue with the application, but allowed a number of us who felt strongly about it, to take it over and continue it. The procedure through Parliament was very slow, and you could feel influence and pressure from the existing Chartered banks, however, Laurentide's application had its own Board of Directors, including several influential French Canadians and it continued to proceed the best way it could. The Senate had a Banking and Commerce Committee to which this Bill was referred. The Chairman of the Committee was a Toronto lawyer by the name of Senator Hayden, who was also a Director of the Bank of Nova Scotia. Months went by and the Committee did not call us for a hearing, even though we were ready, willing and able, and anxious to appear. One afternoon, at 3 o'clock Vancouver time, I was called by the office of the Committee to inform me that we would be given a hearing at 9:00 A.M. the next morning. I explained the difficulty of physically getting to Ottawa by that time, but was told that if I could not do it, there would be no date set for a hearing. I found a midnight flight that would get us into Ottawa around 7:00 in the morning which we took and after cleaning up, appeared in Senator Hayden's Parliamentary office at 9 o'clock. The secretary informed us that unfortunately, there had been a delay in the Senator's plans and that he was not there but in Toronto and would be arriving around noon when we would most likely be able to seem him. He did arrive around 12:30, saw us there and with a minor apology, informed us that he had an important lunch and that he was not able to see us that day, and that a new meeting would have to be scheduled.

After many months of trying, the Laurentide Bank Bill eventually cleared the Senate and so would now have to proceed to the House of Commons for approval. During this time our banking relationships became more difficult. We were asked to supply considerable amounts of information about our customers,

11

DURING MY MANY trips to eastern Canada, Nancy often accompanied me. We had lots of friends, both business and social, and found these trips interesting amongst other things by getting a better feel of what was going on all over Canada. We also visited a number of art galleries and started to acquire paintings and sculptures, which were the beginning of our Art Collection.

One December day in Montreal, we saw a painting at a friend's home whose style was very interesting, and he told us there were several other works by the same artist at the "Dominion Gallery" on Sherbrooke Street. We went there the next day and Dr. Stern, the owner, showed us two of these works. We both liked one of the paintings and I asked Nancy if she would like to have it as a Christmas present. As we were walking back to the Ritz Hotel, a few blocks from the Gallery, I commented that the painting cost as much as a mink coat would have. Whether it was the cold and snow we were walking through, or some other reason, Nancy mentioned that I never gave her the choice. Consequently, on her birthday, which is a week before Christmas, she did receive a mink coat, which she enjoyed, however, after a few years it wore out and ended up in Hungary with one of our cousins where they did not even have worn out mink coats.

We visited Dr. Stern's gallery a number of times and each time he offered to buy back the painting. We bought a number of others from him and enjoyed dealing with him. However, it was obvious that he badly wanted this painting back. One day I was walking down the street in Chicago and saw paintings in a window of an art shop, which reminded me of that "Fujita" that we had bought from Dr. Stern. I went in, asked some questions, and was told that they were by a Japanese painter and when I told them that they reminded me of our "Fujita", they got very excited and wanted to buy it for more than twelve times what we had paid for it. Since we liked the painting, we never took up any of these offers. Many years later, when we had our collection appraised, Sotheby's told us that this painting was so valuable that it required its own alarm. This was going to be too much trouble so we let them put it in an auction in New York where the Japanese telephone company purchased it for a very large amount of money. This turned out to be a very rewarding experience for us, as well as Revenue Canada!

As our Company expanded we not only had the interest in the Common Wealth Bank of the Bahamas, but with our English partners, owned Laurentide Financial Trust in London, England and a controlling interest in Societe Francaise de Financement de Ventes A Credit in Paris, France. Societe Francaise had a very distinguished Board of Directors, which I did not appreciate at the time. When I mentioned to Nancy that one of the Directors was a defunct nobleman by the name of Compte de Riebe, she told me that the Riebe Countess was one of the best-dressed women in Paris. The offices were one block east from the Champs Elysees in Paris where the Company owned a whole floor in an office building. Paris was a very enjoyable city to visit. Here again we bought the odd painting which we have enjoyed over the years.

Our other foreign investment was a minority interest in an Italian finance company in Rome where the President and I became quite good friends. One day he invited me to his country home to shoot birds. He picked me up in the morning in his Ferrari and that was my first experience of traveling at 250 mph. in a car. His home was a very nice country house. It did not have electricity as the line had stopped about half a mile from his property and for some reason it would not be installed for some years. We covered perhaps 20 miles, walking around hunting for birds, sometimes together, sometimes separately. I had a pointer dog with me who would very efficiently stand outside a bush when the bird was in there. I always understood that dogs react to the tone of your voice, rather than what you say, however it seemed this dog preferred Italian because he would not go in to get the bird until the gamekeeper happened to come along and gave him the right instructions.

The head of this Italian company confided in me that they kept three sets of books, one for the tax department, one for the shareholders, and one for their own internal information. Needless to say, they all showed different results. When I questioned him on this, he said that nobody in Italy paid taxes on their real earnings, and if they did, the department would not believe them anyway. As we were minority shareholders and the meetings were conducted in Italian, I had no opportunity to influence these decisions, and was satisfied with the statement we received, as long as the auditor certified it.

12

My first career had come to an end, but I was too young to do nothing, so I took a deep breath and started to look around and figure out what I wanted to do with myself. I was always intrigued by the idea of merchant banking and did discuss this thought with my friends, Rod Hungerford, George McKeen and Bill Ferguson. It turned out that Coronation Credit which Bill Ferguson had acquired our shares, was over capitalized for its business capability as we were once more going through credit restrictions. We formed a company called Douglas Developments and started to acquire Coronation shares in the market. Coronation's President was having a difference of opinion with his banker, who put in one of their senior retired executives as Chairman. When we had acquired enough shares we discussed our situation with these two gentlemen who were not very receptive to being taken over. Their Annual Meeting was approaching and we put Bill Donnelly, a long time associate of mine, on the ballot to become a Director. This was successful and Bill spent considerable time in Toronto where they had moved their head office and confirmed that they did have a fair amount of unused leverage. We then went about and changed the Board of Directors with the co-operation of the banker appointed and appointed Rod Hungerford as Chairman.

Our first investment was a trucking company called Public Freightways, followed by another trucking company in the tanker truck business called Rempel Trail. One of my golfing friends was Jim Methben, General Manager of Johnson Terminals, a large trucking and warehousing corporation. He told me that the principal shareholders wanted to sell, but he was not happy with the potential buyers. We agreed that we would put together a consortium by our group now called Cornat. We would put up the money for one-half of the business and he would raise the other half. As we were pretty small it was difficult to find a banker who would finance us, but our Treasurer made a good contact with the newly formed Bank of British Columbia and a deal was worked out whereby they helped us with the money and we merged our trucking operations into Johnson. Things worked along quite well. I became Chairman of Johnson and found that Jim Methben, while on the whole a very good manager, would not take direction from his Board of Directors. Eventually he sold his shares and his successor, Ron Granholm became General Manager, but with his accounting background he did not give sufficient operating leadership and the Company was not making as much money as it should.

Just around that time, Bill Hudson, who was General Manger of Burrard Drydock, the shipyard in Vancouver and Victoria, approached one of our Directors to say that his Company was for sale. The Company owned land in both North Vancouver and Victoria, a fully outfitted shipyard and had been a consistent money maker. The Wallace family was made up of two senior brothers, one of them a former Lieutenant Governor of British Columbia, and numerous generational members, most of whom worked in the shipyards. The senior brothers decided to retire and sell. On "paper" it looked like an unbelievably good buy and so we went to their bank, Bank of Montreal and asked if they would finance our purchase. Because of the banking bureaucracy, several months went by without having obtained an answer and so, once more we went to the Bank of British Columbia and within a week we had an approval. After we took over Burrard, all but one of the family members resigned and George McKeen became Chairman of the Company, giving a lot of personal attention and getting along well with Bill Hudson. We now had grown substantially and were generating a very good income. The former Bond holders of Coronation, who were all quite nervous with our takeover, had been paid off and various refinancing had taken place.

The dry dock on which ships would be taken out of the water for repair and maintenance was a so-called graving dock in Victoria. It was a long hole in the ground built in 1915, a thousand feet long and wide enough to take the largest ship in the British Navy. However, ships in the meantime had been built with wider beams capable of going through the Panama Canal and these could not be accommodated at the Victoria Yard. We applied to the Government to help acquire a larger floating dry dock, but like so many Government funding applications, we were stalled for a number of years. Eventually it was built in Japan, towed over by tug and is still a mainstay for maintenance and repairs in the North Vancouver shipyard.

At this point, we were approached by the owner of Vickers shipyard in Montreal, enquiring as to whether we would like to buy it. He put a very reasonable price on the facility and said that he wanted to sell because he did not have the resources to issue the required Completion Bonds for the many   projects. We bought it and were surprised to find how much at home we felt in the Vickers facility. Even the walls and furniture were very similar to Burrard. They did not manufacture ships as such, but had a substantial maintenance and repair business on their dry dock and an equally large division manufacturing industrial products such as windmills. One of the interesting products was torpedo launching tubes for the United States Navy. The skill involved here was to be able to launch the torpedo inside the submarine, close off the loading facilities sufficiently, not allowing any water to enter the sub when the torpedo was being launched. This took a special skill, well recognized, but the project was nearing danger when Quebec passed a law that all correspondence had to be in French, a commodity which was scarce in the upper echelons of the US Navy, and they threatened to cut us off. Eventually the Quebec Provincial Government authorized correspondence in English related to this matter.

13

A FRIEND OF GEORGE McKeen's, living in Winnipeg, advised him that a very fine farm manufacturing company, specializing in four-wheel drive tractors, owned by two brother-in-laws was going to come up for sale. We went to look at Versatile Manufacturing, a manufacturing plant under one roof equivalent to fifteen football fields. Four-wheel drive tractors at this time were very much in demand and the engineering, led by one of the two partners, was recognized as world class. They were a strange combination of people. Very strong Jehovah Witnesses which extended to many of their employees. They had a "house" union with whom they got along well, and the operation was extremely profitable. The financial partner advised us that he was willing to sell if we could come up with his price of $27 million (a huge amount in those days) within a week. I phoned our Treasurer in Vancouver and asked him to see what he could do. He was a little surprised at the request, but went to work once more on the Bank of British Columbia, and between them, the funds became available.

We encountered some wonderfully profitable years. For example, one farmer in Australia who I talked to said that he and his brother owned nine of our 12-wheel drive machines worth $500,000 each. Around that time a very popular novel, by the name of the "Thorn Birds" was published. This book took place at a very large Australian farm. We were displaying some equipment in the town of Orange in New South Wales and the organizer of the Fair invited me to come and be his house guest while I was in Orange. I had visions of going to "Drogheda" which was the farm house in the "Thorn Birds", but it turned out that his home, while very nice, was not as elaborate. During my visit I was given a pin with the crest of Orange by the City Council and was surprised that it displayed an apple. When I questioned this, the explanation was the City was named after "William of Orange" and that a key farming product was apples.

A very good friend of mine, Peter Bentley was head of a very large forest company called Canadian Forest Products. He stopped me for a chat one day and explained that they would like to diversify their business and wondered if there was any chance that they could acquire a substantial interest in Versatile Corporation, as we were then known. They were willing to make an offer at a substantial premium to the market for a block of stock, but because they would like to consolidate their financial statement, they would have to obtain 50%, plus one, minimum shares. I discussed it with my Board and we decided that we could take Peter's word for the fact that there would be no interference in management and because of this we would recommend the shareholders tender some of their stock. I told the Bentley's that I would not tender mine unless a small amount was required to give them control, and they were obviously very happy that I would welcome them as partners. True to their word, they participated at the Board level by appointing three Directors and did not interfere with management decisions, but were quite helpful with Policy decisions and certain contracts.

14

As so often happens, the takeover of Versatile Manufacturing hit a few bumps. The former head of Finance, who was the Chairman, did not realize that he no longer owned the Company and made decisions which were not compatible with our policies. We had to persuade him to step down, put on a search for a General Manager and very fortunately came up with Paul Sobrey, who had been the head of one of our competitors. Paul's understanding of the business was excellent and his ability to run the engineering, marketing and manufacturing were first class.

We found that our specialization in niches of the Market worked out well. So when a sugarcane harvesting company in North Queensland, Australia came up for sale, we became interested in buying it. It belonged to, the largest trading company in Hong Kong, and we had interesting negotiations with the principals. The cricket matches were on around that time and several afternoons had to be taken off to enable their top executives to watch the cricket between Hong Kong and England. Eventually we did buy the company and shipped our harvesters all over the world.

15

Over the years I became a Name of Lloyd's of London which means that I participated in some of the Syndicates underwriting a variety of risks. One day when I was in London a war had broken out between Iran and Iraq. Like most wars, I considered this bad news until I found considerable jubilation at Lloyd's, pointing out that insurance rates for ships travelling through the Strait of Hormuz were increased quite substantially that morning. As all things have two sides, four months later I discovered we were having great difficulty in finding a ship that would take our sugarcane harvesters from Australia to Iran due to the risks involved.

One of the nice things I enjoyed was spending twenty minutes each morning with my two daughters. The school was on the way to the office so we had a nice, but short, chance to visit. We also decided that for a few months that we would only speak German in the car. Neither Christine nor Paula spoke German, but as we spoke nothing else, they learned enough that in subsequent years when they went on trips to Europe with their peers, they were able to get themselves by in the German speaking countries.

I was on the Board of the school and was informed that the

junior building, where Paula was at the time, was condemned by the Fire Marshall. I was asked to run a fund raising drive to replace the junior building and reorganize the senior building. I asked one of my friends in Toronto, who ran a fund raising drive for Upper Canada College, how difficult such a project would be and his answer to me was; "very easy". However, experience was proven that between raising money for a boy's school in an old city like Toronto and a girl's school in a younger city like Vancouver, had completely different challenges. In the senior school we also had some Chinese girls from presumably well to do families. Every time I phoned one of these homes I was told that the husband was away in Hong Kong on business and would get in touch with me on his return. Needless to say I never heard from any of them. That was my experience then, but since that time there have been some very generous Chinese in Vancouver, but that did not help my fund raising drive then which proved very difficult to reach my target.

Our 25th Wedding Anniversary was approaching and Paula and Christine decided to throw us a big party. They booked the Georgian Club where our wedding had been held, and sent out invitations to perhaps as many as 100 people. All this was done as a surprise and it was only by coincidence that one invitation returned to the house to Paula was opened by Nancy by mistake the night before, but it all went off very successfully. I must say that on several occasions when I came back from lunch, I noticed my secretary, Heidi, was talking on the phone to what appeared to be Christine in Kingston, Ontario. When I asked if this was a fact, she said yes, but Christine was calling her. She was the coordinator and the two girls pulled it off very well.

Peter Paul and Nancy at dinner in Budapest around 1996. I am
proud of taking these "candid" pictures wile we were listening to
listening to our favorite gypsy music. (For which Peter Paul gave
a generous tip.) Nancy, though only an honorary Hungarian, is
caught up in the rhythm.

Comments added by Alex:

T<small>IME RAN OUT</small> before the whole story is told. I find it impossible to fill in the details, and will not do so. For those who are interested in numbers, I supply just the barest minimum of the business growth. I found the very first balance sheet of Imperial Investment was truly a sheet of paper preserved in a file hidden in the back of a cupboard in Peter Paul's home office room. Next to it were the neatly stacked annual reports of the two companies he founded and grew, one after another. I only give abstracts from the last year of each set that was in this file. They seem to be the last year in which Peter Paul had an interest in these companies.

Corporate Balance Sheets as reported in the year listed

	Imperial Investment 1951	Laurentide 1964	Vesatile Corp 1983
Cash	2,233.13	11,632,801.00	23,362,000.00
Notes receivable	33,755.20	304,073,348.00	14,501,000.00
Shares issued $	11,610.00	34,297,675.00	46,751,000.00
Total Assets	38,445.78	339,262,987.00	673,760,000.00

Of course this does not give any measure of the level of accomplishment. Nor does it report his involvement in charities, Board of Trade, the arts and sports of Greater Vancouver. Or ventures like the Television station or even the Grouse Mountain ski and tourist facility.

On a very few occasions I had a chance to observe his response to charity needs. Just to give an example, on one of my visits to Vancouver Peter Paul and I attended a meeting of the Irish Christian Brothers who were at the time in difficulty with a law suit that threatened the very property of Vancouver College. His response was immediate and substantial. And it was without question.

The one consistent past time that gave Peter Paul pleasure was golf. He learned to play along with our father before we all left Hungary. It can be said that he spent his lifetime improving his game. When Nancy and Peter built their summer house in Qualicum in 1991 it was, of course, near a golf course. The details of building the house were left to Nancy. Peter Paul also had pleasure in watching, encouraging and learning. The result was a true wonder architecture. An open space, full of light, balconies to upper bed rooms, a full view of the ocean from living room and den.

Another life changing occurrence in 1991 was the birth of Julie, his first grandchild. True, Christine did all the work. But she did not deny he parents the pleasures of grandparenting. The fullness of life continued when Mark also came along a few years later.

To carry forward a focus on golf, even in the winter, Peter Paul and Nancy bought a house in Palm Springs, California in 2004. He was very well regarded at his golf club, the Thunderbird Country Club. Christine tells me that he was known at the Thunderbird as the Bionic Man, because even after two hip replacements and a knee replacement he went on playing golf.

On a February evening in 2007 I got a call from Peter Paul while he was vacationing in Palm Springs. He had severe pain in his leg while playing golf. And next day when he played again the pain returned. I thought it was a spasm, and suggested he visit a doctor and get some medication for relief. The next day I got another call. This time it was from Paula. She said there was a diagnosis of cancer, probably of the pancreas. And there was a debate on whether to leave for home immediately or to complete the vacation. I said, "Leave right away and make appointments ahead at the Cancer Institute so that there is no time wasted."

Sometimes being a large contributor to an institute has some benefits because the appointments were immediately forthcoming.

The diagnosis was confirmed. There was no question that chemotherapy and whatever treatments were required were started immediately. But surgical removal was no longer an option.

At the time I was traveling quite a bit to the Midwest of the US on a consulting assignment. I made a series of three legged trips, going to Vancouver before going home. I found Peter Paul, at first very distressed, as expected. Gradually he recovered his composure and became as active as his illness permitted. On one occasion, in the privacy of her kitchen, Nancy said to me, "Peter is terminal, isn't he?"

I said, "Yes. How long he lasts dependents in part on how strongly he fights it."

Nancy's response, "If anyone can fight, it is Peter."

And so it was, for a few months. He gave and received the love of his family, went to lunch with his long time friends and colleagues, visited friends and received people in his home. He drove to church on Sundays, although everywhere else someone would drive him.

His original pain was from blood clots in his legs. That is a characteristic of pancreatic cancer. Spread of the clots is prevented by treatment with Heparin, an anticoagulant. But it is a balancing act because too much drug prevents clotting altogether. Thus at one point there were clots developed in the veins of his kidneys, from which complication he did not recover.

Alex Resumes

Frank

ANYONE WHO CAN count to three will so far have followed the life of only two brothers. It seems appropriate to tell the third story, at least briefly before I continue mine.

While we were boarders at Vancouver College, Frank made a bit of pocket money by doing hair cuts for other boarding students. He showed some creativity, and increased the number of clients by giving a guarantee to correct any gross mistakes. He eventually stopped this venture at a time when he ran for class president and his opponent put up posters saying "Don't get clipped by Frank."

Since we were in different classrooms all through these years I do not know how he got along, except that like all of us, his accent had disappeared by the end of the first few years. I do know that he had some difficult with mathematics. One afternoon I came by his classroom to so that we could do something later together. He was standing there at the blackboard while Brother Murtagh wrote on the board, $a^2 + b^2 = c^2$. And Frank said to him, "That is not fair. You are using algebra to try and prove a concept in geometry." There were other subjects where he was far better than I. He finished four years in Latin, and enjoyed reading the Latin classical writers. Whereas kindly Brother Powers told me after the 11th grade that perhaps I should not plan to do a fourth year of Latin, even if I wanted to be a doctor.

Frank graduated and left Vancouver College with all intentions of becoming a priest. He spent many years at the Seminary and had completed all his studies. There is a tradition for seminarians to wait for what is called a recognized "Call from God" before receiving holy orders. In Frank's case someone had told him that this was essential. But no one had to know what that conversion experience really was.

Frank was too honest to fake such an experience. On the other hand he was not very susceptible to self hypnosis or the power of suggestion. So the calling never came. He looked around and saw others who apparently had such experiences and concluded that he was not chosen. Literally he knew he had not been called. It may seem strange to us now but he did the only thing he could, and left the seminary. He completed the degree in social work that he had started in the seminary and went back to Vancouver to work with the city's social work department.

He was a good social worker, with the interest of his clients always in mind. In fact with a few cases he became very upset that his recommendations for a client were not accepted by his supervisors. He got into arguments with his supervisor and was eventually dismissed from his job.

For many years Frank worked as an independent counselor – psychologist and social worker who charged fee for his service. He also tried his hand at some business ventures. But in truth he did not have either the training or temperament to succeed where tough decisions had to be made. Indeed one frustration we had with Frank was that he could not make decisions.

I was not in Vancouver for most of the years after Frank decided to go into the printing business. He eventually found a niche in printing annual reports for small and mid sized businesses. Here he could advise in layout, format and color schemes. And this maintained him for the rest of his life. Well that is not quite true. There were several times Frank needed financial help. It was mostly Peter Paul who helped him. And I do not know how many times.

Once there was an opportunity to get him to be more independent. It was the rediscovery of the property that our grandfather had purchased in Berlin in 1926. The apartment house was on the wrong side of the Berlin wall. Even so it had been bombed and became a piece of flat land. There was a German historian who made a project of reconnecting such parcels of land with their owners after the Berlin Wall came down.. How he found us is not part of the story.

Peter Paul, Nancy, Peggy and I once met in Berlin after each of us had meetings in various parts of Europe. We looked at the property, and decided that it was not yet ready to sell because developments in Berlin had not yet come to a peak. Yet Frank needed the money now. It was Peggy who came up with a solution. We chipped in to buy Frank an annuity so that he could have a continuous flow on funds for his maintenance for the remainder of his life. It was to be a loan against his part of the Berlin property. That and his government pension, and work he did on the family apartment houses were what maintained him from then on.

It is not totally difficult to understand that someone who never had to worry about money or jobs for the first twenty five years of his existence would not be very good at managing money. There are other responses to exposures equally important in our lives that need to be nurtured and must grow. They cannot start growing at twenty five just because that is the first time of exposure.

But Frank had a different kind of following. Over the years he was involved in a number of religious related adventures. He founded and for years led a group of Charismatic Christians, who met in his apartment or house. I met this group and am convinced that they all had great respect and love for Frank. It was an extended family with numerous connections to both religious and charitable functions all over Vancouver. His understanding in these subjects was strong, clear and unshakeable. He once wrote me a fifty page defense of his position when he and I had a disagreement on a theological subject.

At one time F rank had to have surgery on his back bone. After the surgery he was in a lot of pain. Doctors who never had enough time even to examine him thought the pain was from the surgical scar and gave him morphine. What he really had was a severe surgical infection, and he succumbed eventually to blood poisoning.

There were hundreds of people at his wake. And I was truly touched at the may stories told by people whom Frank had helped in his lifetime. Since I was only a visitor in Vancouver over these last years, this was a side of Frank that I barely knew.

Tough Love

FOR MANY YEARS I did not know the story I quoted in John Mendel's letter. But I became sensitive to a potential for very occasional severe depression in both of my brothers. It was always with sufficient cause. But I have to say that the times were scary. And I reacted sort of clinically to them even though the first time I experienced the need I was not yet a physician. That first time was an episode when Frank came home from the seminary. I deal with it by presenting his poem of depression, below. The next was the time when the Canadian Government turned down the application for a Laurentide Bank. That one I dealt with in four hours in Peter Paul's personal study on Marine Drive, drinking his personal, very excellent Scotch, and arguing long into the night that the world truly had not come to an end. It is truly amazing how resilient they both were in these tough situations. And I feel it as a success of both their lives that they did not permit depression to win them over. There is a last time that I performed that service, in part by insisting that Peter Paul write the chapters that just precede here. The poem, *Tough Love*, below, is dedicated to the memory of both my brothers and it fills in a serious part of our story.

Struggle Through the Night
Francis Stephen Saunders

It was a pitch dark and gloomy night
And dry twigs lay along the path.
Small specks of phosphorous gave a sickening light
But there grew no grass.

There was a muck filled and disgusting stream
And in it flowed no water, but blood that speaks of death.
The air was foul, and hard it was to know
How suffered I when drawing in a breath.

In silent torpor through the night I lay,
Yet knowing not that stillness caused the pain,
And weak from inaction over many years
I found it hard to make a move again.

Then midst this gloomy night a glimmer came.
It faded, leaving little light behind.
But what a hope a little light does give
If for the last ten years a man was blind.

I grasped the hope (the light was gone
But then it came and then it went again.)
And so I tried to move but found it hard.
By indecision I was nearly slain.

But glimmerings of light, they still must come,
And I will try my eyes to open wide
To see the many mirrors that reflect the Son,
And one bright mirror is right at my side.

The mirrors and the Sun, they both are bright.
The Sun would blind you if you dare to stare.
But when you look away you see the night,
For rays of light must be diffused by air.

And groping then without the aid of light
A move is made; -- and then to my delight
A whiff of freshness came my lungs to soothe.
The way is always there, -- ignore or choose.

And when the air has once again been known
It spread all light beneath the Son's great throne.
And things, which in the night, one dimly felt are there,
Become reality in the daylight air.

When I first read the first two stanzas of Frank's poem, I said to myself, "I know this place." It is the trail to the senior camp at Elphinstone. But I also knew the place where Frank was coming form when he wrote it, as you can see below.

Tough love·

I know a place where, even on a dare,
Brave men won't go. It's called despair.
Battles there are fought with meager odds
And only fools rush in to fight false gods.
I am that fool. Perhaps the only one
Who could have fought that battle,
    And I won.

God was not false. There is no other,
His silence at one time betrayed my brother.
In the seminary he was doing fine.
Before commitment there he sought a sign.
A sign from God that he belonged.
It did not come. And he was wronged.
Some holy fool had said it must be so.
And he concluded that God said, "No."

So he came home. And then one night
Expressed his fears to me.
From some ascetic height
He had descended to that pit.
It was pitch dark, and he was caught in it.

There was no way out that he could see.
I said to him, "You listen to me!"

He let me commence.
I scolded him right there for arrogance!
How arrogant must a person be
To say to God, "You owe a sign to me.
A personal sign that I can recognize.
And forever it would be my prize."
Depression may be treated with a shock
This did the trick. I saw the jail unlock.

And I heard him say,
"Thank you. I had lost my way."

No one knows when depression may hit.
Even the strong may succumb to it.
No one supposed
My other brother could be so disposed.

A man who built himself from scratch
To a success very few could match.
A wife, two children, all amenities
A lead figure in many charities,

Uncountable friends, his life in order.
Respectably, he was growing older.
One day a doctor said it plain;
"That is cancer causing your pain."

At home he sat in his favorite chair
He did not move except for dining.
And suddenly he slipped into despair,
His spirit dead, his body slowly dying.
All visitors were suddenly denied.

Like a fool I rushed to his side.
He trusted me, and so I tried.
I tried it all. Even invoked his pride.
Whatever reason, he just balked.
Then I suggested a little walk.
He saw that he could.
I said that he should.
That was the crack!
Little by little, his spirit came back.

I gave him back to his kids and wife
For four more months of a good life.
(My trick; No matter how grim,
I showed that I believed in him.)

I do not write for your belief.
I write just to relieve my grief.

Margit

I WAS VERY PRIVILEGED, at UBC, to have Earl Birney as a creative writing professor. On a memorable occasion he read his famous poem, David, to the class. Among many items of advice that Birney gave to his class, was an idea that one could often learn the trade of creative writing by imitating an expert. The following poem is a shameless imitation of Birney's style and even picks up the theme of the dilemma that was posed by that Poet Laureate of Canada. This seems to be a good way to start in again on my story, because it begins to carry out my promise to speak of people who influenced me a lot. And it tells of the direction I took after my last chapter.

Margit
I.
The summer when I was five
I invaded her kitchen to steal
A handful of raisins.
Right fist tight, I made for the door,
And then I saw her. Smiling, she said,
"Smart guy, Sándor,
Can you count your fingers?"
On my left hand I started;
"Egy, kettő, három ___ ,"
I knew the Hungarian numerals well.

"Go on," she said. And I did.
When raisins peeked out on "hat," (six)
She laughed away my guilt and said,
"Don't steal. You can always ask Grandma."
And I did; many times that summer.
I still love raisins,
And Grandma.

II.
The summer I was eight
We vacationed in Zurich.
Mother pleaded for Grandma to join us
But she loved the
mother country too much.
We never returned. But I wrote her
From Zurich and Melbourne, and Sydney,
And Vancouver, for ten years.
Her address was always Budapest.
They told me the letters were censored.
What did I know? War is hell!
I escaped. She did not.

III.
The summer I was eighteen
She finally came. A Swiss watch
For my graduation. I still have it,
And wear it, and remember.
She gave me time; her time;
Whenever I asked Grandma.

I marveled at how she learned English
In giant, incredible strides, while
I struggled to learn chemistry and math.
"Smart guy, Alex,
  you want to be a chemist?"
"No, Grandma, a doctor." I said.
"Tell me about your teachers." she said.
  Right then I started, knowing them well.

And my courses. The ones I liked and
The ones that were downright boring.
"Go on." she said. And I did.
And I marveled at her insight while
She laughed away my frustrations.
"Don't fret.
You can always talk to Grandma."
And I did; many times as a student.

IV.
Some weeks before my wedding
I told her about George.
Left over from the "drug lab";
A white rat with brilliant red eyes.
Clean and smart, a good house pet.
He could climb my pant-leg
To sit on my lap, or stand straight up,
Sniffing the air for strangers.
"Pfft!" he would sneeze when angry.
But time was unkind as he aged.
Now he was too weak
to climb without falling,
And he lapsed from his clean habits
At the carpet's expense.

On my fingers I recounted for her
His remaining good traits
But she took my hand and closed it.
"End it gently," she said,
"His brain is already dying."
My fist was tight now in pain,
But I knew she was right.

V.
It was some months later. She called
"I'm so upset," she said, "I can't write."
In minutes I was with her,
Pleading to take her to medical care.

But she loved her apartment too much
To leave now. Next morning
There was no choice. A weak right arm,
And she could barely stand.

VI.
It is hard to recall how long
That stroke imprisoned her,
Unable to speak, or to move her arm.
I marveled at how she tried again
To speak even a few words.
On my hand we counted my fingers,
But the words would not come.
And she closed my hand tightly,
Looking at me with brilliant eyes.

VII.
One day I brought my son to play
On her bed.
She knew we were coming.
Her left fist tight, she played
The counting game with him.
As he opened her fingers, counting,
He squealed with joy, discovering
A handful of raisins.
Her laugh was as brilliant as her eyes.

VIII.
Her doctor called me once.
"___ a bad infection developing."
He said, "We could treat it with sulfa.
But I want you to visit her first."

IX.
She held my hand as I talked
Of the passing world.
Then she closed my fingers,
Gave back my hand

And looked at me
With bright and feverish eyes.
My fist was tight now in pain,
But I knew she was right.

X.
We said that she died of the fever.
And all the bereaved were consoled
Because her brain was already dying.
And all remembered her from
The time before her stroke;
Her incredible insight and strides.
But I will remember how
She taught me to count,
With a handful of raisins.

Lake Louise Revisited

THERE IS ONE small part of Peter Paul's story on which I would like to expand, since it was my very small contribution to his business. It happened that during the last summer that I worked at Lake Louise, Peter Paul was for a time vacationing in Jasper, 160 miles away. One night at a staff party at Lake Louise I met up with Bruce Lee, a bell hop, who was one of the first investors in Imperial Investments. After a few drinks at the party he told me that he had just carried suite cases down to their car for some people from Los Angeles who were planning to go to Edmonton by way of Jasper. They had planned to look for oil investments in Edmonton. As it happened the bell hop knew their name. When I heard this story, at around 10 PM, I left the party and started to hitch hike to Jasper. I arrived there at about 4 in the morning, found the cabin where Peter Paul was staying and knocked on his door. As surprised as he was to see me we spent about an hour making some plans. Then we rested for a few hours and went to breakfast.

At breakfast we paged the potential investor by name in the dining room. When he answered the page and came to us, we invited him to breakfast with us. There was an incredible discussion that I did not completely follow, but Paul Kirby left us at last, knowing that there were other opportunities in Canada besides oil. As Peter Paul tells in his story, this $10,000 was the first substantial single investment, and it was a boost to the growth of the company.

Paul Kirby himself was very satisfied with his investment. As

I recall, 10% of his investment was in preferred shares. These were eventually sold some three years later for $150,000. In this situation, therefore, everybody was a winner.

But that is not the end of my interaction with Paul Kirby. He became a very good friend of the family. He especially liked Grandmother Margit, and every time he came to Vancouver as a visiting composer and orchestra conductor he would call on Grandmother. Many people knew of their friendship.

One evening when I was visiting Grandmother she received a telephone call from a mutual friend who told a puzzling story. Paul Kirby was at the Vancouver Hotel and was seen to be very loud and disruptive in the lobby. There were no details. Grandmother asked me to go there and investigate, and I did so. Peggy was with me.

When we arrived at the Vancouver Hotel, there was no sign of Paul Kirby. I went to the guest registration and asked. I was told that he had been there and had indeed caused some embarrassment, but that he had left an hour or so before we came. I asked to be shown to his room and eventually to be let into his room. That is where we found him, lying on his bed, asleep I thought, but I could not wake him. I searched his room. In the night table I found a hypodermic syringe and all the tools needed for Insulin injections. When I pulled these out for better examination Paul roused himself for a moment and said, "Of course!" in a very loud voice and then was immediately unconscious again.

At this time I was in third year of medical school. I knew enough about insulin shock that I realized Paul was in trouble. But I did not have the confidence to help out all alone. So I called one of my clinical instructors, a Dr. Victor Herzman. Dr. Herzman instructed me over the phone and I got Paul to swallow orange juice laced with sugar. Over about 15 minutes I got the whole glass of juice into him.

And so it happens that the first life I saved in my medical career was the life of a friend!

Over the years, as I watched Paul Kirby conduct the Vancouver Symphony Orchestra, I caught a very subtle movement. While conducting, he would very smoothly reach into his coat pocket, and then his hand went to his mouth, without missing a beat with the hand that held the baton. He had learned to deal with his need for sugar, when the insulin overacted during the strenuous effort of conducting.

At the same time Dr. Herzman was my clinical instructor I was seeing a most interesting patient in the clinic of the Vancouver General Hospital. She had been in the clinic for over 10 years, and had always told the same story. But the story was most bizarre and she had never been believed by students, interns, residents or even the clinical staff. I honestly believe it was the way she told the story that made doctors lose patience with her. As a student, I always felt I had a lot to learn, and because of my problem with Dyslexia, I may have been a better listener to verbal communications. At any rate, a few weeks prior, I had heard one of the professors of surgery, Dr. Al MacKenzie describe this exact condition. So I was as prepared to hear her story as anyone ever was. It turned out that she had an extremely rare tumor, in an extremely rare setting. I was permitted to assist with the surgery, and also follow the patient over some years. Eventually, Dr. Herzman and I published the case history. It was my second publication as a young doctor. I believe it was the first for Dr. Herzman.

It may seem strange, how such things develop, almost by chance, but the fact that I had publications before completing my training and specialty work was a strong influence on my being a successful candidate for a teaching position at Stanford University.

But now, once more, I am ahead of my story.

Starting a Career

WHEN DOES A career really begin? Is it after graduation and after all training is finished? Is it, perhaps, at the time when one has insight on what one's career should be? That insight can come at almost any age. Or is it when the stirrings of curiosity become so strong that they are almost unmanageable. That is where, in my opinion, a research career starts. If I am right, then nurturing that career in research is an obligation for the child's care givers. Nurturing is an "oh, so subtle," activity that perhaps it even may not be a conscious act.

No matter what the intent, the one who first nurtured my curiosity was my Uncle Stephen. He had a term he used; "You figured it out!" Perhaps I used it first with him, but he consistently responded with it as a form of praise. He did so even if I did a dumb thing with a budding technical understanding. For instance, I once fixed the lights in the farm house when the fuse (an old fashioned fuse that screws into the receptacle) burned out. I fixed the lights by putting a penny in the fuse receptacle and put the old burned out fuse back on top of it. Yes we got the electricity back because I figured out that the fuse was just a circuit part between the electric supply and the house current. But it was an ever so dumb trick overall, because the real function of the fuse was to prevent an overload. I learned that from the farmhand, who told me the danger of what I did.

The farmhand, Walter, was another inspiration, since he never let anything stop him from his tasks. He once told me he could likely fix an airplane also, as long it worked by principles that could be discovered by study. In some ways that may sound arrogant. But what he meant was that everything works by sound principles. One just has to have the courage to "figure them out."

The Irish Christian Brothers at Vancouver College were an amazingly nurturing group of men. In my first year at VC my fifth grade teacher was a Brother John Maloney. I know his first name because when we played basket ball, Brother Reilly would call him by first name when he wanted the ball passed. "John, pass me the ball". But when little, short, me had the ball they stood back and let me try for the basket. Brother Maloney was quite upset for a while that I could not read in fifth grade. He thought it may have been all the traveling and change of language. So he had the whole class IQ tested just to find out where I fit in. He came to me and said that it is OK that I could not read at that time and that it will come. He said he expected me to be at the top of the class sometime later. So it happened. There were three of us, year after year who vied for first place. The insight of not flunking me for my reading failure was a tremendous leap of faith.

There were only five of us as seniors (yes it is a giant leap forward in time) who had an interest in biology. So we developed an after school-hours program with Brother Victor Castle volunteering to put together a curriculum and be our teacher. I think we learned as much as any other biology course even if our teacher was learning at the same time as we. I confirmed this when I got into University and could tell how the other students were prepared. Brother Castle was also the choir master for the whole school. It is hard to tell how it happened, but four out the five who took this biology course were the members of the Quartet who sang from "Handel to Haarlem" for Brother Castle. At another concert we covered "From Bach to Boogie." In fact the four of us had a scholarship opportunity at Gonzaga, Spokane (Bing Crosby's old school). But one Quartet member, Dick, decided to go off to the Seminary instead.

The fifth member of the biology class could not sing at all. He had a chronic cough, which we watched deteriorate over time. Watching him was another true inspirations. I just had to try to figure out what was wrong with him and how to cure him. The time for that had not yet come. Jack inspired, both in his acceptance of suffering, and in the potential for improvement in doctoring that just had to happen over the extent of my career. By the time I graduated from VC I knew the career I wanted.

I applied to two colleges. UBC was one, and the other was Royal Roads military academy. I felt that the military may give me a scholarship all the way through medical school if they once saw how dedicated I was. Two of us from VC went to the examinations, interviews and health exams at Royal Roads. We both passed the exams and the interviews. In the health exams it was found that I had "joint mice" in both my knees. My class mate had joint mice in his shoulders. I was turned down because my medical classification prevented me from marching like a soldier. My class mate, son of an admiral, was accepted and went on to a most distinguished naval career himself.

At UBC, the first two years, it was the chemistry teacher (who shall be nameless) who did me the greatest favor. His lectures were so boring that I decided to apply at Stanford University as a transfer student. There were entrance exams to be taken. Since I was working in the Canadian Rockies that summer, I hitch hiked down to Calgary where I had arranged to have the tests administered. I later received a letter that I was in the upper 85% of those who took the tests. Welcome to Stanford.

Well, Stanford was a different story. I was never bored. In fact it was a struggle to keep up because everyone in my classes was competing to get into medical school. Organic chemistry was a tremendously tough subject as I viewed it. It turned out that the reason for it was that I could not just memorize structures and reactions. I had to figure out how it all worked. And so I did not get the top grades. But I have been able to make better use of that chemistry than most of my class mates. Dr. Bill Bonner, who gave the second quarter course in organic, and also directed the laboratory courses was especially inspiring. I once went to see him in his office, to ask if I could take his special course in Carbohydrates. I looked past his inner door into his laboratory. It seemed a very busy place. I made a comment, "Is this what you do in your spare time?" And he just growled at me, saying, "I teach in my spare time!" I told him the reason I wanted to join his class was because I had a friend who is suffering from a disease where carbohydrates (Mucous) was drowning him in his lungs. And I wanted to understand how such people could be helped. Years later, when I was also a teacher at Stanford and was marching in the graduation exercises I happened to be marching alongside both my organic chemistry professors. They not only remembered me by name but told me about adventures in their classes that I had, myself, hoped to forget. For one thing, I wrote the same paper for two classes. Oh I had permission to do it, but the two classes fit so nicely that they remembered the result.

One class was Dr. Bonner's Carbohydrates. The other was a lab course in Coastal Invertebrates. I decided to study the mucous coat of Sea Squirts, whose technical name is Tunicates. It was the tunic that was made of mucous. And it was, indeed a carbohydrate. A sugar polymer. So I wrote a paper on the analysis and got A in biology. And an A+ in carbohydrate chemistry. It was the only A+ I ever got in college! Thus you can imagine that it had some influence in helping orient me towards my skills.

Stanford was really full of adventures. I only joined two clubs. While at UBC I had been in 8 clubs and each told me that one night a week should not hurt my studies. The two Stanford clubs were the Camera Club and the Newman Club. It was through the Newman Club that I met a girl friend who worked in the chemistry laboratories as a student technician. In fact she worked in the lab right next to Dr. Bonner's, and I was impressed. One evening when I came to pick her up (forget where we were going) she was late because she had to finish some calculations on her results. After watching her calculate for a while with an ancient hand crank calculator I told her that in my Bio-Statistics lab I had access to a calculator that could do all of this work in just a few minutes. Naturally she accepted the offer. So we went off to the Stat Lab and did her calculations.

When I was finished, I said to her, "By the way, you are using the wrong statistics."

The word got back to Dr. Art Rinfret, her boss. And the next time I came to visit, he and I had a long discussion. He gave me a pile of raw results, and said, "Here, do the statistics. See what they mean."

I had the advantage of a Biostatistics library, and a "fast" calculator. The problem was one of rat endocrinology. It was about the growth of a gland and what it secreted after injecting the hormone that Dr. Rinfret was working to purify. But the problem was generally like that of vitamin dose response. So I applied statistics from that other field. I came back and showed Dr. Rinfret that the same hormone was causing both a secretion from and the growth of the same organ. He then said,

"I have been trying to show that for three years, and I will be damned if I know how you figured it out!"

Uncle Stephen was ahead of his time!

Art Rinfret asked me to stay with his lab. He eventually offered me a position to design his experiments. And he would pay my way through a PhD in Biostatistics. As it happened, this was the same week when I got my acceptance letter from UBC Medical School. What to do? Another professor of biochemistry, Dr. Clark Griffin, whom I and my girl friend had befriended, advised me that if I do not go to medical school I would never forgive myself.

I did get one other gift from Art Rinfret's laboratory. I got to marry his technician! See how love life and career intertwine! And right up to the present writing, I still help Peggy with statistics when needed.

During the first three years of my medical school I remained in contact with Art Rinfret. I did his statistical analysis without pay, just as a friend. I followed his career even after he left Stanford. He went as a senior scientist to Union Carbide, in their Liquid Nitrogen Division. Art did some truly innovative work with making red blood cells stable to freezing so that when they were later thawed out they were not broken up by the freezing, and so could be used for transfusions. His process was used as a life saver in several war theaters. It may still be in use, I have not lately followed the field. Unfortunately Art later had a nervous breakdown. His old technician, now my wife, and I visited him during this time and he was ever so pleased to see old friends. He was never able to come back to a creative scientific career.

Dr. Clark Griffin not only expressed an interest in his students, he acted on his interest. At one time I had to have surgery to remove a bone tumor from my hip bone. Dr. Griffin was so concerned about the results that he asked to have the biopsy also read by a pathologist friend he had at Baylor University. Fortunately everyone confirmed that the tumor was benign. Dr. Griffin left Stanford before I came back there to teach. He went to Baylor Medical School as professor of Biochemistry. He was there for a very long time but recently I have lost touch with him. But at a time when I was on a speaking tour for a company where I had made some medical products, I wrote ahead and he came to my lecture. The lecture had a considerable amount of biochemistry in it, and so I dedicated that one lecture to my old professor. He did not get away completely unscathed. I told a story about him, in how he sometimes had lab parties where he used 100 % alcohol (200 proof) and flavored it with concentrated orange juice and cooled it with dry ice. What a punch! What a professor! As I said, my years at Stanford were eventful.

There was just one more story to tell about Stanford professors. Dr. Hubert Loring was a professor of organic chemistry who gave an advanced course in nucleic acids. His whole course about the chemistry of the nucleus of cells dealt with how to break down the large molecule from which chromosomes were made and to analyze these sub components. It was a terribly frustrating course. We kept saying to Dr. Loring that there must be a function to this beautiful natural reagent. His answer always was that the most important thing was to understand how to take things apart and understand the components. That was in 1953. It was approximately the year that Watson and Crick, while working on the same molecules by X-ray diffraction and other means discovered the basis of the genetic code. A few years later people had learned not only how to take the nucleic acids apart, but also how to build them up. From then on the field flourished. Anyway, I think I was in the last year when Dr. Loring gave his nucleic acid course. But of course Stanford has remained at the forefront of the field both in genetics and in chemistry.

No matter how difficult Stanford was, it barely prepared me for medical school.

Career Confusion

L IKE MANY OTHER people who go to medical school I went because of a dream. That dream was that I could do something that would cure many people. Not just save lives, but make people's lives more tolerable. Medical school was a means to pay my dues, so I could practice and find a place to accomplish the dream. The path turned out to be indirect. That was true for many classmates. But it was not obvious at the time. Paying one's dues involved courses that did not seem like they were on the straight path. But the theory was, and is, that any practitioner of medicine has to be exposed to it all because one never knows which knowledge will be useful. As Professor Sidney Friedman said to us on the first day of his Anatomy lectures,

"It would be OK with me if you never took this class, except that some day, after I have had an accident, I would look up form my stretcher into one of your faces and would say to myself, 'My God! He does not know his Anatomy!'"

There were classes that I thought in the beginning were going to be boring, but actually turned out to be fascinating. One such was Histology. This is the study of anatomy at the microscope level. This is where the structure and function came together for me. It truly helped me understand. The microscope was just the intermediary. The tissues and organs were cut up into very very thin slices that fit onto glass slides of a standard size. Then the slices, called sections, were stained with some chemical methods that made individual features stand out in good contrast when looked at through the microscope. In this way not only was the structure clear under the microscope, but the chemistry associated with the structure was also clear. I learned that the histologist called this feature of microscopy Histochemistry. And the people who specialized in this were called Histochemists. It was something to remember as careers developed.

In the same way as each student shared a cadaver with five other students, we also had a box of slides. The cadaver was destroyed during the year of our study. The slides remained for the next year's class. But the slides were always available for our examination. So when we studied some item in Biochemistry or Physiology courses and it referred to a microscopic feature I could go back and understand how the two were related. Making those connections was far more important for learning and remembering than plain memorizing. Wherever possible I took this approach to learning.

Our class in the University of British Columbia Medical School was just the fourth class since the school began. The dean of the medical school, Dean Weaver, told us we were his "graduating class." With us he was in his fourth year in the school and in our first year the very first class would be graduating. There was indeed a sense of freshness in the whole school. Some of the professors were not much older than our classmates and their experience in teaching may not have been very long. Certainly each of the basic science department heads had been new on the job four years earlier. Yet one has to say that the courses were all well organized and there was very little wasted time. We students were very impatient in the first year to meet up with patients and with disease processes. But that was not the way things were done at that time. The focus was on getting the basic sciences out of the way so students could then focus on the patient and the art of diagnosis and healing.

Thus we were even given a "thesis" to write in the first year. We were expected to do some original work, just like in a PH.D. program. I took my "thesis" seriously and actually did a piece of original research. Most of my classmates chose a path of doing an original library study in the field that they thought was close to their career objectives. But I did not know that or care about it, since Professor Harold Copp in Physiology was willing to give me a little lab space and let me have some rats for my experiments. It was, of course, an experiment in

Carbohydrate chemistry. In this case the carbohydrate was Vitamin C. I had read some papers in Dr. Bonner's class at Stanford on how vitamin C was synthesized by most animals, but not by humans. Humans are deficient in some feature and so we must have the vitamin every day or so or we get a disease called Scurvy. To prove the point of that synthesis I concluded that one should be able to divert a precursor sugar in rats by feeding them a compound that would be detoxified by the precursor. I planned to produce Scurvy in rats. It took about two months of feeding a compound very similar to Menthol. It worked. The vitamin C concentration in the rats went from a normal level to essentially undetectable.

I was so pleased with the results and was planning my report to my classmates as we all had to do for our thesis. Just the day when I was to make my report I went for a final look in the library to see what I may have missed. There I found a brand new journal article that someone else had thought of the same biosynthesis pathway, and had proved it by isolating the proteins, the catalysts that were responsible. I had been scooped! I reported it just that way in my class. Dr. Copp pointed out that the thoughts behind my work were quite correct and that I had done the work without knowledge of the other scientists. He accepted my "thesis". In that class, I picked up a key word. Dr. Copp had called me a "scientist"! That was enough for the day.

I will not describe the classes or the struggles we all had in learning. Rather I would like to describe adventures along the way. In the second year after one of the pathology classes I was speaking to Professor Hal Taylor. I asked his opinion about an experiment I was thinking of getting sponsored by another professor. Dr. Taylor turned it around on me and asked me to do some work in his lab that dealt with a subject remotely connected to carbohydrates. It was a simple experiment in wound healing. He was thinking of using special stains to detect a class of compounds that should be present in healing wounds. I happily accepted to work in his lab just for the experience. I developed the methods for him. At this point I had learned a number of special staining methods and applied them to a new piece of work. We did demonstrate that one of this class of compound was present in healing wounds. It had not been done before, and Dr. Taylor reported it in a scientific meeting and also we wrote a paper on that work. When it was finished, we had come to the conclusion that one of these compounds, called MPS was present in healing wounds. I asked Dr. Taylor which of the 5 compounds in this class he thought was present in the wounds? I still remember his answer;

"What do you mean, which one?"

Clearly Dr. Taylor was interested in the mechanics but not the chemistry. To me the chemistry observed at microscopic level was very interesting. I read a lot about both the MPS compounds and about Histochemistry, although it was not part of our class work. I learned that there is a general back ground structure called ground substance in which all cells of the body are supported. In a healing wound this ground substance is made by the local cells that first come in to do the repair. This is the same material that goes wrong in arthritis and a whole group of related conditions. I became interested in both the chemistry and in the disease conditions and Dr. Taylor encouraged that interest.

We had developed a relationship. It was Dr. Taylor who took the initiative on my graduation to invite me into his Pathology program and suggested that I should become a Pathologist. And I did. Once again I am ahead of the story.

Just in passing, one question on one of our Pathology exams was about how cancer cells spread to other places. The standard answers, of course were that they are less strongly attached to other cells of their kind and therefore can move away easily. Also they can more easily invade into the ground substance and are therefore not limited in their location at all. I had also read that cancer cells can secrete a catalyst that breaks down the ground substance, and this catalyst had a specific name. I decided to add this specific knowledge to my answer. I was marked wrong for it by the associate professor who was correcting the papers. I went and showed him the article from which I got the information but he said my answer was wrong, nevertheless. I told this story to Peter Paul, and he told me that it happens all the time. Professors do not have the whole story. How could they? All fields were getting more and more complex. He had had the same experience, many times. When he knew he was right he just ignored the professors who marked him wrong. I know that some of them in later life admitted that he was right, and that they had held some economic theory in error.

The clinical years of medical school are a blur in my memory. That is not because they were without adventure or insight, but because there was just too much. I got immersed in the both the learning and the actual practice of diagnosing and treating real patients. It was a reality of becoming a doctor. But there was always an uncertainty. Is this what I want to do with the rest of my life. It would be so easy to make that positive decision and go on after the commitment. For the time, I acted as if that decision had been made. That is all that made sense.

What Else Develops?

U P TO THIS point I write as if personal life had been put on hold. To a certain sense that is true. The commitment to study and learn to practice were sufficiently demanding that most of my classmates and I were completely involved. But it is not, and cannot, be entirely so.

The individual who graduated from Vancouver College and entered a life outside of institutional borders had done so by acquiring book knowledge. I had very few positive assets besides school learning. I had no knowledge of manners, of personal interactions, of caring for myself financially. I knew that I was missing a lot, but did not yet know what those things were. So I took the attitude that I must learn by adapting and by learning from my mistakes.

I mostly entered situations that required no long term personal commitment. That was certainly the case at Lake Louise. There were hundreds of college age youngsters from many parts of Canada who were more or less in the same situation as me. We were all far from home, possibly for the first time, and ready to experiment with personal interactions. At College I first joined a variety of clubs ranging form the Social Problems Club to the Player's Club (Green Room) and the Newman Club. Eventually I weeded out all but the Green Room and the Newman Club.

The Player's Club was an entirely new experience. It was a group of amateurs who put on plays for the University of British Columbia. We had the use of the very large Auditorium and stage, and all the back stage utilities, including, of course the Green Room. That is the name given to the room where actors relax before a play begins. We used it as our club house. The excitement for me was being involved in managing a whole enterprise, with the motto "The show must go on!" We did all the decisions of what play to put on, planning the whole season, stage props, sound, lights, as well as the acting. The play was usually presented at the University at the end of a semester and went on tour over the Christmas holidays to places like Penticton, Trail and many other places. Each of these was a one or two night stand. And the arrangements were that the players were housed with local families. This whole enterprise essentially paid for itself. We were not in it for the money. For me it was a way of learning many new and wonderful personal interactions with a group that had clear common goals.

I tell only one story about my Player's Club group. Two of the strongest performers, let us just call them P and M, were also personally involved. It made their acting even more credible when they interacted on stage. They played some very mature roles, such as "Who is afraid of Virginia Wolfe?" And they were thrilling to watch real close up, both in planning and in performing. Eventually, of course, they were married and I lost contact with them. That is until one day when I was an intern at the Vancouver General Hospital, they came into the Emergency Ward where I was assigned. Their 3 year old daughter had an accidental fall and had a cut right over the bridge of her nose. What a tragedy! Would it ruin her acting career? Look at all the blood! P and M were all worked up about it. And then they saw me. There was nothing for it but I must fix their child right there! And they, hovering over every stitch. I did the stitching under the skin and pulled the wound together in an exact text book manner, but with great care, and without putting a needle through the skin to leave a scar. Three weeks later they came back to me to show me the result. I could not even find a small scar. This episode was a true source of temptation to go into practice. The emotional reward seemed so strong!

The Newman Club was an adventure of a different sort. They had a small hut in an out of the way part of the campus, behind the main library. Their main initial attraction was a place to have lunch every day with people I got to know quite well. They had a variety of programs that helped maintain our connection with the Catholic Church in an environment that was otherwise completely without any religious or ethical or moral influence. It was the same for everyone who joined. And as such it became a strong support group. Thus when I left UBC and went to Stanford, the Newman club was just about the only club I joined.

For a very brief time at Stanford I also joined the Foreign Students Club. This was just to make sure that I had not missed some item that all other foreign students should know. But by that time I had completely lost my accent. The members of the club called me "foreign student from Texas", implying that I really did not belong. I accepted that opinion and left. And that is how I happened to spend a considerable time with the Newman Club at Stanford.

Unlike the club at UBC, at Stanford the Newman Club was housed off campus, because the university founders had desired to have a totally non denominational environment. That was OK because almost everyone at Stanford had access to a car. The house in Palo Alto had been donated by a famous writer, Kathleen Norris. There was enough room on the grounds to also build a chapel. And that Chapel was a true work of art. It was filled with paintings by a French artist, Andre Girard. The whole chapel was a memorial to Ann Brokaw, daughter of Clair Booth Luce, who had died in a car accident. Anyone who had been introduced to that environment was strongly attracted to it. Then add to it the popularity of the resident priest, Fr. John Tierney, and students away from home were guaranteed to return. Fr. John would have breakfast for students after Sunday Mass. He always finished a meal by patting his stomach and saying "God is good." Then the students planned activities that included Sunday beach parties at Santa Cruz, volley ball in the back yard and other outings.

At one of these parties at Santa Cruz I wandered off for a brief time to examine the base of the tall cliffs right behind the beach. The bottom layers had sea shells embedded in the rocks. As the ocean waves eroded the rock the shells became visible. I had not taken any courses in Geology and so it was a marvel for me to see. Then suddenly I noticed a girl from the Newman Club next to me, examining the same rocks with a very intelligent order. She was going from upper to lower levels and making careful note of the differences in shells. We started a conversation, and she explained a brand new field to me; how layers of sediment can be interpreted. I also found that she was taking the same courses I was taking in chemistry and had even taken a biochemistry course. And she was now working as a technician in the research laboratory next to that of Dr. Bonner. And that is how I met Peggy Bouvart. After that the Newman Club became even more interesting, for both of us. Peggy has remained in my life ever since. Perhaps at another time I will write the true love story, but this is not a tale of romance, so on we go.

Peggy came to Vancouver to work as a technician in the medical school after my first year there. She got to know the family, and we took a year to make plans and had a wedding in the St Ann Chapel at Stanford at the end of the second year of medical school.

There were quite a few married students in my class. In some way they formed a society of their own. But the overall camaraderie in the school was much stronger. Every one knew every one else, had worked with them, and played with them. Beside school we did have social events. Like poker nights, and weekend parties. And meeting in the downtown taverns just for fun. One evening at a downtown pub that shall remain nameless we were having our usual drinks and a waiter came by to ask us to leave because we had a black man with us. He was a class mate. We were shocked! But I asked the waiter to count the number of our classmates present. Told him there were four classes of 60 students who would listen to us. If we left we would not come back. And that was my only exposure to that kind of discrimination. And we put an end to it in two sentences.

One major social activity was the "Medical Ball". The third year class always provided the entertainment. Our class decided to put on a musical play in the Gilbert and Sullivan style. It was called "Dr. Bunthorn's Bungles." The star baritone was Ron Hancock who played a surgeon - and later became a very good one. We wrote the play and rehearsed twice weekly for ever so long. Jim Cousins was both rehearsal pianist and accompanied us in performance. Bernie DeJong had the most marvelous tenor voice that could be heard above every one, especially in the quartet singing. We recorded the dress rehearsal and the record is still being played at our reunions. As the play unfolded Dr. Bunthorn states that he had never lost a case. "What, never?"   ---
-   "No, never!"   ---   "What, never?"   ----   "Well, hardly ever ---"
And then there was a parade of the individual case histories. Josh Goldbloom had a natural limp that was used to illustrate an orthopedic failure. Since we were studying case histories and how to write these,

the story writing was a lot of fun. Dr. Bunthorn decided to change careers to psychiatry in the Finale Solo. And the medical staff and graduates at the Ball were almost as much entertained as we were.

A year later we graduated, and went our separate ways. As it happens, there were many successful surgeon and psychiatrist careers among our class mates. The bond within the class remains to this day. We meet at reunions. We meet and we sing. And we tell stories.

Beginnings of focus

ONE OF THE secrets of medical education is that Interns learn a lot form nurses. As we examine patients and write our histories at the ward desk and then write our prescriptions for the incoming patients in the wards, the nurses look over our shoulders. Without seeming to do so they use their long experience in advising what those prescriptions should be. A little shake of a head may indicate a potential mistake. I just have to say that it was an important part of my learning. In part it was because the attending physicians were very busy. They came by in the mornings and got reports on patients, visited the ones that were most serious and then left for their office practice. It was up to the interns, and their senior counterparts, the Resident Physicians who were going on with their specialties to fill in the remainder of the day for all patients.

There were a few staff doctors, mostly our professors from the school, who were full time at the hospital and clinics. I will tell one adventure with one of these doctors in a just a little while. But the major task was to show that we had learned enough in each specialty to be general practitioners. And that was not too difficult. We also learned that patients have special needs and personalities. For example, a patient with severe pneumonia may also be a drug addict. Should the intern treat the addiction? I found out from a sincere patient whom I did my best to cure of both, that he had no plans to stay clean once he left. But thanked me for my effort.

There is one International event that greatly influenced my intern year. It was the 1956 revolution in Hungary. They thought that with some help form the USA they could throw off the Russian Communist rule, and so a revolution started. But the help did not come. Many in Hungary lost their lives. Many more fled the country. Many of those who escaped at that time settled in a small town some miles up the Fraser River, called Chiliwack. And those who were sick in that community often found their way to the Vancouver General Hospital. There it became known that I could speak Hungarian. And so I inherited a large patient load that I would otherwise not have seen. I learned a lot. But it was difficult, since I only had an 8 year old's vocabulary in Hungarian. Could one imagine asking sensitive questions of a Psychiatric patient, a paranoid who thought everyone was persecuting him (perhaps they were, for all I knew) with an 8 year old memory of language. Or how should I ask about the patient's last menstrual period, when I barely remembered the word for blood? So I became a conduit. Doctors would be with me in the examining room and coached me on the questions to ask and I just had to try to communicate.

I have to say that there was no specialty in that intern year that I did not like. But except for the excitement of the action in surgery there was nothing that greatly excited me as a career, except perhaps treating children. Even that, I felt was a sort of altruistic attraction, and not a real reason for making a decision. However, during that year I had developed some further associations in the Department of Pathology. I was beginning to do some research with two of the younger professors. Both were British origin and worked well together. One was a surgical pathologist, Dr. Philip Vassar. The other was a super technician whom Dr. Hal Taylor had invited to bring a new capability to his department. This was Charles Culling. Charles was a specialist in all the techniques of preparing tissues for diagnosis. He had written a book in the UK. And hence he brought a reputation with him. The three of us began to work on new methods of tissue preparation. And I eventually wrote another three or four papers with them during the next few years. Dr. Taylor, simply took the attitude that I was going to join his department. One day he simply came to me in the dining room and said. "Alex you should put your name in for a resident position soon. I expect you will want to work with us in Pathology." It was a logical continuation. And I did so that very day.

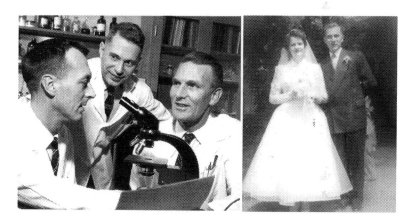

Dr. Phillip Vassar, (new) Dr. Alex Saunders and Charles Culling 1959
Peggy and Alex, May 21, 1955

However, there was one experience that helped in my long term career, although at the time I did not know exactly how. This happened just before the end of my intern year. Professor Mack Whitelaw was a senior member in the Department of Medicine. He had a research project of treating cancer patients with some of the drugs that were just then becoming available. In fact I do not know if the drug he was using was on the market at the time or if he was doing a clinical trial. For some reason that I no longer remember Dr. Whitelaw asked me to help him in this trial, and I treated eight patients under his guidance. The idea was to treat them with the drugs and watch the secondary response of their white blood cells. The white blood cells that fight infection respond almost as much as the cancer cells and we had to stop treatment before those white cells were lost. To give the quickest summary; all 8 patients died, just at the end of my intern experience.

At the beginning of my Pathology residency I had the task of performing the autopsies on seven of the drug trial patients. The eighth patient died in Victoria and was lost to our history. The puzzle was that we had acted and reacted according to the protocol . When the reported blood cells were low we slowed the treatment. When they were high we treated more strongly. At autopsy, I found that all 7 patients died of infection. Without intending to do so, we had over treated them all. We had killed off too many white blood cells.

In the department of Pathology Dr. Taylor had established a library of specimens. Every microscope slide used in a diagnosis was kept for a defined period. The slides on which the differential blood counts were done on these seven patients were therefore available to me. The autopsy investigation gave me opportunity to look into these patients with detail. And I set out to investigate how we had been misled in our treatment. I sat down with my assigned microscope and performed the counts myself. The idea is to search on the slide for the first 100 white blood cells that come into the field of vision and classify them into the 5 well known kinds of white blood cell, then record the results. It took about 6 minutes for each slide I did. Then just to be sure I had it right, I did all the seven slides again. And I went back through the several weeks worth of slides and did them all twice. Each time I did the same slide I got a different answer! Was it just because I was not experienced? I did a few slides 10 times. And each time I got a different answer! By this time I was confident it was not lack of experience. The technique was faulty. To explain in simple words, it would have taken ten times as long, or an hour for each patient, to come close to a serviceable, or statistically reasonable result. And that was not realistic to expect of any laboratory. I made a promise to myself. If ever I had the opportunity I would do something about this situation.

Professor Whitelaw agreed with my autopsy conclusions. The drug was dangerous to use without a further way of monitoring patients.

Not all of my Autopsy work was accepted with such grace. There was, for example the incident of four patients from the cardiac ward who had the same specialist. Each patient had had the same clinical story; a moderate heart attack. It was important to have the heart as much at rest as possible, so the nurses were given discretion on how and when to use Morphine to alleviate pain and to calm the patients. During the next two weeks or so an episode occurred where the patients became restless, and tried to get out of bed. They could not express themselves, and the nurses used their discretion to give some morphine to calm the patient and he or she went back to bed. In twenty minutes or so the episode was repeated. And again in another twenty minutes. And then the patients expired.

At autopsy the same findings were very clear in all four of the patients. Their hearts were healing as good treatment had been instituted. They did not die from their hearts failing. The common feature in all four was that their urinary bladders were very, very full. I showed the results to my supervisor. He agreed that the four autopsies should be separately summarized but delivered to the attending doctor as a package. When I did so, the attending physician came storming over and said "Are you implying that these patients should not have died?" Our answer was simply. "All we do is make observations, Doctor. You have to reach your own conclusions about how morphine depresses the will to breath."

But we did not see any more patients with a similar history at autopsy in the next two years. So we believe that the situation was corrected. In case anyone reading here has wondered, that is how autopsy pathology is intended to save lives. It obviously is not the life of the patient who is at present on the autopsy table! But I should quickly say that such episodes are not very common.

Much work at autopsy is for the purpose of establishing normal patterns. Also one can observe trends toward disease. The most obvious one is the gradual change of arteries, even from a very young age. And the other trend that really stands out is the accumulation of dust and soot in the lungs, and how that is increased in patients who smoke. I became interested in whether the tars from cigarette smoking could also be found in the lungs, and for this purpose I took my samples to the research laboratory where Charles Culling had a fluorescence microscope. Both Dr Vassar and Charles Culling became interested in the question and we followed it for some time in both autopsy samples and in the coughed up spit of volunteers. We did find fluorescent tar, and it was strongly concentrated in some cells.

Brightly shining cells of the kind we recognized as scavenger cells. To our surprise we found some such cells even in a few volunteers who were not smokers. One technician in particular, who had volunteered, and worked in the our lab, had these cells. We even showed them to her in the microscope. And for days we grilled her on her smoking habits. She denied ever having smoked at all. Then we found that she had had a cold. She had taken a tetracycline antibiotic. When we got some from the drug store we did indeed find that the drug was also fluorescent and in the same color. But that was not the end of the story. We found that even in patients who smoked, it was not the tars that were fluorescent in their cells. It was only those smokers who had also taken tetracycline who had fluorescent cells. And the number of such cells related to a probability of developing a cancer. Using some chemical tricks I showed that we could tell the difference between the tetracycline and the tar fluorescence. The tetracycline fluorescence disappeared when the slides were treated with iron or aluminum. This was the kind of "Histochemistry" or tissue chemistry that became my long term interest. I had plenty of time to both do my residency work and stay attached to the Vassar – Culling laboratory. And it was this relationship that enabled me to publish another few papers before I ended my training at the Vancouver General hospital.

Please observe a subtle change in the last paragraph. Now it is "we found" or "we discovered". What I personally discovered that was very important to me was that working in a team was a very powerful way to advance a project. It was Charles who initially had the experience with a fluorescence microscope. I learned the basic techniques from him and applied them to a new question. It was Dr. Vassar who had the long term experience in Pathology and knew which cells we were seeing with fluorescence. My contribution was the original idea and to show the difference between the two fluorescing substances, the tar from smoking and the drug that concentrated in the same region where to tar was expected. So we found something new and unexpected. It was truly "we" found it.

Another example of the "we" was a consultation that was referred to Charles Culling by Dr. Taylor. A Japanese company, who shall remain nameless asked why their microscope was having sales problems. People were complaining of headaches when using their binocular product. Charles spent about a week, off and on, trying to find out why. He did confirm that everyone who used it found the images very good but indeed had headaches after some use. When he asked me to evaluate it I looked and thought that I would like to see everything just a bit larger. So I replaced the original eye pieces that were 10 times magnifying with those of our Zeiss microscope that were 12 times magnifying. The result was astounding! No one who used that combination had any headache or eye strain. Then I turned the trick around. I returned the original eye pieces and substituted the objectives from a Leits Microscope. These are the lenses closer to the slide. The same happened. No headache. We then evaluated both sets of lenses to a German microscope. It happened to be a Leits microscope. Here we found that the consult client's eye pieces worked best with the Leits objective. The final conclusion was that the Japanese client had copied the Zeiss objectives and the Leits eye-pieces. It was like performing an autopsy on a microscope. And the result was a financial success for the client. And we truly saved people from a lot of headaches!

Incidentally there was another new "we" that happened late in my intern year. Our son, Paul, was born. And now at home there was "we three". And that was another totally new experience. It is now 52 years later and the children and grandchildren, are still a new experience. Gradually there was "we three", then "we four" and for a long time it was "we five". More lately we are now up to "we ten" plus some in laws. Each of us has a story much like what I am telling here. Perhaps a bit more protected.

In my career development I next did something unusual, perhaps against the advice of Dr. Tailor and others in the Department of Pathology. I decided I wanted to have some more detailed exposure to a focused field of basic science. There was no one at Vancouver who could provide that, so I applied and got a post doctoral fellowship in Chicago. I had been following the work of a statistician, a Dr. Dorfman for some time. When I applied to the University of Chicago I applied to Dr. Dorfman. But it turned out they were brothers, Ralph and Albert. I ended up working with Albert, in a small institute called La Rabida. And it was not statistics, it was the detailed chemistry and immunology of the MPS carbohydrates that was of interest. This was the same MPS where Dr. Taylor had said "What do you mean, which one?" There are actually five main kinds that I learned about in detail. More than that, I would like to tell about a truly strong scientific team. Anyone who had the experience of working in that laboratory came away with the same conclusions. Science is fun. Science is worth the effort. Science does save lives. And none of it is worthwhile without personal commitment and interpersonal great expectations.

La Rabida, University of Chicago

A T THE BEGINNING, I knew that I needed an entry Visa to the USA. I had been there as a student, and could not work to earn money. Returning now was different. I needed to support family and perhaps would stay for an extended period. So I went to the US Immigration service in Vancouver. There we started in on the paper work and an official was filling it all out for me. But Peggy came just to help if it was needed. The official very quickly told me that I was a Hungarian National, and that the US quota for Hungarian Nationals was filled for the next four years. We had a brief discussion about it, saying that my wife was a US citizen. To no avail. The official was about to close his books when I turned to Peggy and said, "Peggy, please tell this man that you are a US citizen and he cannot treat you like that." There was an immediate and impressive transformation. Papers were quickly filled out and the Visa was granted, along with a Green Card. That and the eventual; Social Security Number have been with me ever since.

We sold our car in Vancouver and rented our house to Charles and Mary Culling, flew to Chicago and quickly found an apartment close the workplace. La Rabida was on the lake, in Jackson Park, which was a large green area. It was the weekend of the fourth of July, and we would have had a few days off before starting, except that one of the staff at La Rabida knew we were coming, so we were invited to the fourth of July party at her house and met everybody and their wives before I even went to the office once.

On the evening of July third, Peggy and I went for a walk in the beautiful green park that was just three blocks from our apartment. Very soon a police car drove up. The police man came and talked to us. He said we are obviously new in Chicago. No one ever walks in the park in the evenings. It is too dangerous. That was our introduction to Chicago. We often walked, but always toward the stores after that evening.

Across the green park and on the lake-front was a building from another Era. It was built to look like the monastery where Queen Isabella of Spain commissioned Columbus to sail in the Nina, the Pinta, and the Santa Maria, on his voyage of discovery. After the world fair and exhibition the building was given to the University, which was another 15 minutes drive from the lake, and at the other end of Jackson Park. A building of about equal size was attached by the University, and that was the institute where I worked for the next two years.

Albert Dorfman was a pediatrician of some stature in the University. His reputation was about equal to that of the department chairman (whom I never met). Instead of running the department, however, Al chose to have his own separate little institute on the lake. I feel he had the best of all worlds in academia. He did not have the headaches of the department chair, but had a little empire just the same. And he did not have to deal just with other pediatricians so he built his own staff. He did see children as patients, but most of them were in his sub specialty of Rheumatology. Al was a true leader in science. And a wonderful person to everyone of his staff, from his secretary to the facility engineers as well as technicians, fellows and senior scientists. I was told that I reported directly to him and that he would assign my projects. But he next very quickly told me that I had access to all the senior scientists and that my project would get me involved with a good number of the most experienced people in the field. He understood that I was interested in the chemistry as it applied to tissue analysis. But I could do that sort of on my own, since that was not his groups expertise.

What was planned was a complete project. I was to study the immunology of one of the MPS molecules. I found out that they were not just carbohydrates, but some of them were attached to proteins. And therefore people could become immune to their own tissue components. And that was the immunology to be evaluated. To do so, I was to purify the compound, make it very clean by chemical manipulations, and then do the immunology experiments on rats.

To give the magnitude of the task, the raw material was to be from the slaughter houses of Chicago. I was to take the central cartilage from the nose of cattle after their heads were cut off. I did the dissections on some 30 of these heads, and came back to the lab to clean and mince the cartilage. It took about three weeks.

Then I worked with Marty Mathews, who was both a carbohydrate and protein chemist. He taught me cold room techniques, extractions and all sorts of tricks. And the purification went on for about 3 months. I also worked some with Anthony Ciffonelli. Tony was a true carbohydrate biochemist. He knew both the life science sugar polymers and the organic chemistry that enabled him to do the very careful purifications and chemical analysis. He was taking the large molecules apart and establishing the repeating units of how they were put together. Mostly I learned the methods of analysis used in the laboratories in the whole institute. Tony was also known for his sense of humor. It could play out in the middle of a serious conversation without any warning. And everyone enjoyed his company.

Tony had carefully explained to me how he got interested in carbohydrate chemistry. He said that as a youngster he had worked in a bakery. On occasion he would put his finger in the raw dough and then taste it and lick it off his finger. Several times he liked the dough quite well and went back to stick his finger in it again. Then when he came back to look at the dough later on, it had liquefied. Tony said that is how he discovered for himself that his spit contained something that had a powerful chemical reaction. Of course we know this as the enzyme called amylase that breaks up starches into simple sugar. But for Tony it was a world wonder, and he built his career around that early experience.

By now my own project was going along well. Al Dorfman also introduced me to the chairman of the Pathology Department at the medical school, and I went every week to their seminars just to keep in touch with the whole field I had chosen. They were quite different than the seminars that Al Dorman himself held at La Rabida. On the one hand, the focus was on diagnosing "difficult cases". On the other it was in presenting new ideas from the literature and discussing the on going activity in each laboratory. Since the main thrust at the institute was on arthritis, we found ourselves one day discussion back pain. One of the other post doctoral fellows, Dr. Jerry Gross thought that much pain was caused by the "drying out of the cushion between the individual back bones, called vertebra. This cushion is a disk between the vertebra and is mostly made up of one of the MPS and a structural protein. Tony Ciffonelli said he had often thought about making an analysis of the cushion between backbones, but he did not have access to the specimens and also that dissecting them out was very difficult. My comment was that in the Pathology department I could get access to the specimens at autopsy. And dissection is just a routine task. At this point Al Dorfman interjected a sort of cynical comment. He said,

"Dr. Cifonelli, meet Dr. Saunders. Dr. Saunders, please meet Dr. Gross. It seems that together you have the solutions to a problem that could be solved."

And so it happened. Arrangements were indeed made to obtain specimens through the Autopsy department. They were delivered to the laboratory assigned to me. I did the dissections and passed the pieces on to Tony. Jerry Gross also took part in the analysis, and eventually wrote the paper which was published in all three of our names. We did indeed find that the main kind of MPS in the discs of older people was the kind that did not draw in water and so the cushioning action failed. We asked Al Dorfman if he wanted his name on the paper, since it is his institute. He said, no, his only contribution was to bring us together and then things happened. From that experience I also learned that there are catalysts beyond chemistry. A catalyst can be described as an agent that brings other items together and permits things to happen that would be energetically very difficult otherwise. Usually the catalyst is not used up in the process.

Jerry Gross had done most of his work in the laboratory of one other senior chemist. That was Dr. Sarah Schiller. She had worked out a method of separating and analyzing MPS from tissues without the use of big chromatography columns like Tony Cifonelli was using. Her method was not as rigorous, but was far more practical when large numbers of specimens needed analysis. This method depended on precipitation the MPS in combination with a special reagent. Then by adding salt to compete against the reagent the MPS would come back into solution one by one. This was just like "titrating", which was one of the simplest methods all college students learn in first year chemistry. It was a simple and elegant method. And so the adjacent laboratories hummed along, mostly independent. But every once in a while a common problem arose and then people blended smoothly to a common benefit.

Dr. Schiller's actual project was to treat rats with various hormones and see what effect it had on the MPS of tissues. She found that there were indeed effects. For example, she found that one of the MPS, called Heparin, was increased in both diabetes and in thyroid deficiency. This in turn got Tony Ciffonelli more interested in examining the structure of Heparin. And one of his findings I thought very strange. He said that in the structure of heparin there are 2 ½ sulfate residues for each disaccharide repeating unit.

My comment to Tony was, "God does not do things by halves."

Sarah Schiller who heard the comment agreed that the final explanation would be something else.

As time went on I began to think again of how to apply what I learned to the field of Histochemistry. I decided that it was Dr. Schiller's elegant work that could best be applied. That was a thought to put aside while the activities at La Rabida continued.

In April of the second year of my fellowship I asked Dr. Dorman if I could go to the meeting of the Histochemistry Society in Atlantic City. He said I should go, and that we should give a paper on the immunology studies I had done to the Federation meeting held also in Atlantic City the week after. I looked at my personal schedule. Peggy was to deliver our third child in the week after the first meeting. We talked about it at home and both Peggy and Al Dorfman said I must go and that it will all be OK. I drove to the meeting. It was a long drive but less expensive than flying.

It happened that I was just a bit late for the first really interesting paper. I entered the presentation hall and stood just inside the door in the semi darkness while slides were being shown by one of the most respected leaders of the field, J. Everson Pierce. I had a copy of his book and had read much of it. About two minutes after I arrived, another late comer entered and stood in the back beside me. Looking over to him, I saw a man slightly older than I, with flaming red hair and full beard. He wore a slightly faded blue suite coat, a tartan shirt, baggy trousers, and his socks did not match. He listened carefully to the speaker. When the talk was over, this red headed wonder marched right up to the podium in front, pointed his finger up to Professor Pierce, and said very simply, "You are wrong!" And then he proceeded bit by bit to dissect and demolish the presentation. The whole audience was spellbound by this event, and it turned out that in the end Dr. Pierce had to concur gracefully that he had made some errors. When he returned to the back of the hall I somehow found myself talking with the read head. We went to lunch and sat together and talked about the subject some more. I no longer remember the subject of the paper by Dr. Pierce. But my introduction to Dr. Leonard Ornstein was memorable. Every time I went to the annual meeting of the Histochemistry Society I made a point of finding him and chatting about our work.

On the drive home from the meeting in Atlantic City, there was a rare springtime snow storm. Somewhere in Ohio, it got so bad that I simply had to go off the freeway and find overnight shelter. Meanwhile at home the time had come. And I was not there to help Peggy. She had the presence of mind to call the police for help. And so she was delivered to Lying In Hospital, the obstetric ward of the University of Chicago medical school by a police car with sirens blaring. Very shortly thereafter she delivered our third child, our daughter Joanne.

At about the same time I wrote a letter to Dr. Hal Taylor saying I had a successful fellowship experience and was ready to come home. Dr. Taylor wrote back to me, saying he could offer me a post doctoral fellowship if I would come back to his department. I showed the letter to Dr. Al Dorfman. He said I should write and say I have had a better offer. I said, "But Al, I don't have a better offer."

Al said, "You deserve to move up at this time. Don't worry. If you don't find a better offer I will keep you here for another year."

He then called the chairman of Pathology at U. of Chicago, who knew that Stanford medical school was looking for new people. It was arranged that I should interview at the Histochemistry meetings. The man I interviewed was a professor in the Department of Pathology at Stanford. He had devoted his full career to Histochemistry, and was in fact a chemist, not a pathologist. His name was David Glick. The whole interview spun around Dr. Glick telling me about his work and how he had spent years studying a certain cell type called a Mast Cell. This cell was known for containing Histamine, the allergy related hormone, and Heparin, the MPS that Tony Ciffonelli had just dissected chemically. I got a turn to speak and showed him some new things about heparin.

Also showed him that in terms of Pathology the Mast cell is related to one of the white blood cells. A bit of information he had missed. And finally told him that I cannot match his numerous publications since I was still at the beginning of my career. I only had seven at the time. But three were in the field of Histochemistry, and how to apply it to Pathology problems. He said he had never known a person at the end of Pathology training to have more than one or two publications.

David Glick gave me one piece of advice before we parted. He said I should concentrate effort in the next few months on applying for a research grant so that when I arrived at Stanford I would already be funded. And that is how I got an offer to join the Leland Stanford Jr. University Department of Pathology. I did apply for a grant from the National Institute of Health to work on the Histochemistry and Pathology of MPS. The grant was funded by the time I started at Stanford. I had all intentions of returning to Vancouver and Dr. Taylor's department. But, indeed, I had obtained a better offer.

A Department in Unexpected Chaos.

THE FIRST WEEK at Stanford, in July of 1962, was spent in getting to know the faculty and the layout. I now had my own office, with empty bookshelves, a telephone and a Dictaphone for dictating my autopsy reports. There was a desk and two chairs. I also had a furnished laboratory, with no equipment in it. There was a supporting staff who were pleased to order my equipment and took care of all those types of details. And for the first time I had a real Salary! I wrote to Peter Paul in Vancouver and told him how wonderful it felt to have started in on a career. And he was ever so pleased to share my enthusiasm.

Peggy was also very pleased that we were back, home. And she spent some time introducing our children to their grandfather.

Composition of the Faculty was a bit of a surprise. There was a chairman, Dr. Alvin Cox. Half of his time, at least was in running the department. There was David Glick, who was a senior professor with tenure, but who did not have a pathology practice capability, since he was a chemist by training. There was also a senior professor of pathology whose interest was the history of medicine. At one time he had given lectures in the department but now was fully devoted to history, and since he had tenure, he could not be moved. Thus he was not to be counted on to either take a role in the autopsy room or to teach students during the school year. There was also a senior doctor who had control of the Surgical Pathology sub-department. He had succeeded in separating himself from the main department, in terms of function and of income. And he did not see any reason why he should do any research or teaching. Thus the mandate for all faculty performing three tasks, teaching, practice and research was a good theory at our department but no longer the way the department functioned.

Dr. Al Cox had a solution to his problems. He hired three shining new junior faculty. And we were to do all those things that his senior, tenured faculty, were either unwilling or unable to perform. I met the other two in that first week. All three of us were in our first faculty positions. And we became good friends. We did indeed solve the department's problems. In doing so, we did not recognize how much we gave up in our own academic careers. I may as well tell right now that all three of us spent the next seven years carrying the load of obligations, and were then told that we did had not performed sufficiently to become tenured. And at that time it was "up or out". The situation was not much improved by Alvin Cox resigning as chairman after my first year in the department. He decided that he would end his career as a member of the dermatology department. We thereafter had a series of "Acting Chairmen" all of them were visitors, and not permanent faculty.

We each made the best of the situation. Even with all the work, it was a period of growth for each of the new faculty.

Having never lectured to medical students, except to my own classmates in reports that we all gave, I set about to develop those methods during the first teaching quarter. In this the greatest help came from Al Dorfman, who had told me at one time, "Just remember, you know ten times as much about the subject as those who are listening. It was true. The students wanted to learn form us. All we had to do was organize our lectures. I did rely heavily on text material, but eventually prepared my own set of slides. Slides were not easily come by in those days. They were made on paper and then photographed. But it was worth doing. As I got into it and organized my own material, Al Cox saw that I was supervising the department photographer for my needs, and he assigned the photographer to report to me. Aside from the technicians I hired for my research, this was the only person who reported to me over the time I was in the department.

Well that is not exactly so. I did have a post doctoral fellow. He was in a fellowship funded to David Glick, in Histochemistry. He wanted to do a specific project in MPS and so he became part of my grant's research team for two years. I also had medical students who wanted to work in research labs. And they were assigned in accordance with their interests. So there was usually at least one in my laboratory over all that time. There was also a high school student, Jon Sumida who one day appeared and said he needed no pay and just wanted to learn what research was about. I gave him projects that were informative for him, but not necessarily in line with our main thrust. Jon eventually became a professor of history. In a book he wrote on a semi technical subject he very nicely gave me credit for nudging him in a direction so that he did not fear the science field, although he was not meant to be a scientist.

Service mostly included supervising residents in their performance of autopsies. There were a few interesting cases, but as expected, most autopsies are routine. Patients died after their doctors had done whatever was possible for them and there were very few surprises. In the few exceptions it was possible to write and publish case reports. Of this the one that stands out most was the autopsy of the first heart transplant patient at Stanford. I did not disagree with the surgeon who gave the news interview on the patient. According to the surgeon, the patient had died of a fantastic galaxy of complications. But he had lived long enough to show the possibilities in the surgery. And he may have lived longer, if the laboratories would have had the methods to track the complications as they developed. The surgeons had capabilities more advanced than the laboratories.

In my own research I began by developing the Histochemistry method based on Sarah Schiller's method of separating MPS. I did not physically separate them, just showed that in microscope slides I could identify one separately from another by the salt concentration "titration" method that she had developed. In stead of the precipitating reagent that Sarah had used I chose a fluorescent dye that had the same general chemical structure as her compound. I was able to show that the fluorescence disappeared from slides as the salt concentration increased. And in concert with her original work I showed that those that were increased in Thyroid disease and Diabetes by her test tube analytical methods also were increased right in the microscope slides. And this was true not only in the rat experiments, but also in patients.

And so I accidentally came back to evaluating Heparin in the tissues, right in the individual cells where it was synthesized in nature.

I must stop describing the science for a moment to describe the esthetics of fluorescence microscopy. Mast cells stained with the fluorescent dye were like looking at a deep red sunset. There were faint but brilliant green structures around these cells in the tissues of the rats I studied. In lower salt concentrations there was a faint orange haze over the green, as if they were clouds in the sunset. These were the MPS of the supporting tissues. They disappeared from view at higher salt because of the titration effect. As I increased the salt even more I expected the sunset appearance to also change and disappear. And eventually it did. But sooner in some cells than in others. At this point I remembered my discussion with Tony Cifonnelli.

There are 2 ½ sulfates per repeating unit of Heparin.

No Tony, God does not do anything by halves.

It was right there in front of me. Some cells contained Heparin with three sulfates per repeating unit. Some others contained heparin with only two! When the tissues were extracted into test tubes the distinction disappeared because the extract contained both three sulfated and two sulfated heparin. Hence Tony was right, on the average. But in this case average is the wrong statistic.

And my image of God survived.

That method was in part inspired by David Glick. In the past David had designed methods to measure very tiny amounts of chemicals in a large number of ingenious ways. He had never done this particular task, but I was encouraged by his work to measure the content of single cells under the microscope. I designed methods that worked in a test tube just to know the chemistry was right. And then I designed my own microscope measuring system with light sensor (and a lot of detail not needing description here), and then passed the method on to Sylvia, my technician, so she could measure hundreds of cells, one by one, in the microscope fields. That was "aspirin time". It was a truly tedious method. It was possible to do perhaps 30 cells in one hour.

I forget how the next stage started. Someone said to me that down in the basement someone was measuring cells at very high speed and I should investigate it. I went prowling through the basements until I found the laboratory. It was run by a geneticist, Dr. Leonard Herzenberg. How he got the fast measuring equipment is a story in itself. It was called the Blue Machine because it came from IBM. An engineer, by name of Louis Kamenski had designed it as an entry of IBM into the life sciences business. And there were three prototypes of which Leonard had one to evaluate. Leonard had a project on several immunological cell types but the instrument stood idle often because its throughput was remarkably fast. So I was allowed to learn to use it and then to do some experiments using the Blue Machine.

The results were that I repeated three moths of Sylvia's work in one afternoon, since I had kept all of the raw materials. Not only did I repeat that work, but instead of 30 cells for each experiment I had 10,000 cells measured for each! And sure enough, God did not do things by halves. There was heparin with 2 and other heparin with three sulfates for every repeating unit.

I submitted a paper to be read at the Histochemistry meeting that next April. While I was reading the instructions in the Journal of Histochemistry on how to submit the abstract I happened to see an advertisement. A company in New York State was advertising for a person with a Masters Degree in Histochemistry. The task had to do with being able to stain white blood cells. In my letter to the company I wrote, "I know what you need. A person with a masters degree will not be able to help you. But I can."

There was a phone call from Tarrytown, New York. How do I know what it is all about? It was an engineer, who was project leader. I explained that there was an enormous need for an automatic and accurate differential white blood cell count. If they were not developing it, then they should be. We had a few more conversations and on the last one I was asked what salary was needed to go to Tarrytown? My response was likely a bit higher than for a Masters Degree person. The engineer said he will call me back.

There was no response for three weeks, and I thought I had lost the chance. I was also interviewing at four universities for faculty positions and had developed two offers. I told one of them I would respond after the Histochemistry meeting. Then the engineer called me back and told me that they could not afford me. I decided to still wait till after the Histochemistry meeting but called the chairman who had made the offer and said I am likely to accept. Please wait just a few weeks till after the meeting.

The paper I prepared was both a conclusion about Heparin and about how to use a flowing stream to make rapid individual measurements of chemistry in individual cells. The Heparin story had implications for how better to purify this important substance that had a strong role in keeping blood form clotting. I had every intention to follow up and do that work when I continued my own research. It happened I did not get that chance. But others have done so, and there now is a very potent injectable drug for people who have blood clotting diseases.

After I presented my paper in Atlantic City, I was sitting at the bar of the hotel with Leonard Ornstein. I wanted his opinion because he had told me not to get involved in measuring single cells. I asked him directly why he had said so. His response was that he knew that it was a difficult and new area. If I did not have enough persistence I would likely fail. I had been afraid that he was going to march up to the podium at my talk, point his finger at me, and say I was wrong. Instead, he told me at the bar that there was a company in Tarrytown that would be very interested in someone who had my approach to cell analysis.

I told Len that I had already called them. That after the snow storm in March they had called back to say they could not afford me. He told me that I had just talked to the wrong person. And would I mind if he made a few phone calls for me? I said I would not mind. But just now, let's have another drink. We did, but he made the call anyway.

When I got back to my hotel room there was a message, saying to expect a limousine to drive me to Tarrytown the next morning. I was to meet with Mr. Jack Whitehead, the president of Technicon. I had seen the earlier products of this company. The main product of which I was aware was the Autotechnicon, a tissue processor that enabled technicians to prepare tissues for making very thin slices. I had not been terribly impressed with the product. The fact that it had a rigid, programmed cycle of activity made it difficult to do innovative things. But I was curious, and was ready for the morning Limo.

When I met Jack Whitehead, and a Director of R&D, Hy Mansberg, I was told that more recently the company had developed a method of measuring chemical samples one after another. The secret was in placing bubbles in the flowing stream so that one sample did not get mixed up with another. One reagent after another was added to the flowing stream and light sensors did the measuring at the other end, when the chemical reactions were complete. It was called continuous flow chemistry. The inventor was Leonard Skeggs, a chemist who worked with kidney dialysis instruments.

I said that it seems that it should be applicable to the analysis of cells, and that I had worked with a flowing stream method for the analysis part, and had just given a presentation of the results. Hy Mansberg said, "We know. And we have the same idea to combine the techniques."

Then I asked if they were by chance working on a differential white blood cell count? The answer came with hesitation. And in confidence they answered "Yes." But then Jack Whitehead went on and said "But we can expect you to keep that confidential because we want you to come to work for us."

The chance I had promised myself as an intern was at hand. How could I solidify it? I was totally without experience at this kind of discussion. I wished I had had a chance to call Peter Paul and ask his advice. But what I said was, "Your engineer already told me that you cannot afford me."

Jack Whitehead responded, "See this office? I make the decisions here. And it is my money. I expect to make a lot more money on this investment."

Just to get ahead of the story again, Jack Whitehead waited until my project was nearly complete and then he took his company public. Then he said, "Overnight I have become a billionaire!"

When I called Peter Paul and told him I had accepted an industrial job, he told me I should have asked for shares in the company. I told him it was part of the package.

And that is how I left full time academic life and the practice of medicine. But not research. I had found a way to be both in science and in business. But I had to figure out how to make it work.

Jack Whitehead, in a gracious move, told me that I could continue my academic connections. I did that by also getting an appointment at New York Medical College, department of Pathology. That is where I kept the equipment I had received from my Stanford grants. The part that has been most useful for me, and I still have is my microscope. I continued to lecture on the diseases of MPS, especially on the inherited diseases all the time I was at Technicon. And I took part in the academic life of the department.

Tarrytown

I WAS ALMOST LATE for my first day of work at Technicon. We arrived the night before and staid the night at the Holiday Inn in Tarrytown, just about a mile form where my new job was to be. That was the day of the first moon landing of the US Astronaught. I was up until late hours watching this event.

The house we had picked out was not ready and we lived for a few weeks in a motel in a small town called Ardsley. It was cramped and not too pleasant, but Peggy did the best she could to keep the children busy while I got started in my work. The wait was worthwhile, because the house we purchased in Bedford Village was just right for us. It had been built by an architect to his own liking. There was plenty of room and the feeling of openness in the middle of a forest of maple trees was a never ending change of view with seasons. The out doors was not yet well finished. I recall that on weekends, when no one had made plans, I always said, well if no one has plans, we shall all go and move rocks. We eventually made a beautiful rock wall. But we also spent many weekends with a great variety of local activities. Bedford Village was another 20 miles or so north of Tarrytown. That made it close to 40 miles to downtown New York. We went to the big city on a few occasions, but life was really satisfying in the Village. There were many families with children the same age as ours, and we quickly made a lot of friends. There was also a resident group who had been in the Village may years, and we were told once that the "new comers club" was open to all for 15 years after their arrival. I personally did not find it so. There never seemed to be a distinction. No one asked how long we had lived in the Village.

It was about a half hour drive from Bedford Village to the offices and laboratories of Technicon. But the drive was on easy highway and there were spectacular views along the way of forests and low hills and several man made lakes. I was never bored on the trip, and only had trouble with it a few times in snow. I had become a "commuter".

My first title, as I came to work at Technicon was "Chemist". I was to be an advisor to the project run by an electronic engineer. He, in turn, reported to Hy Mansberg, who reported to the VP of Research and Development. So I enthusiastically looked at the science of the project. And there were several surprises.

It was, indeed a project for creating an automated white blood cell differential counter. I was finally in the right place. The project was populated by several engineers, both fluidic and electronic, and there were two consultants. One of the consultants was the one who had created the concept for the project, and he was frequently at the laboratory looking at progress. To my surprise, the other consultant was Leonard Ornstein, who was Professor of Histochemistry at Mount Sinai Hospital and Medical School.

The project could best be described as a combination of imaginative biology and faithful support from the engineers. The basic idea was to make some kinds of white cells "eat" iron particles, which made it possible to pull them out of suspension with a magnetic field, and permitted the counting of the remainder of the cells. In addition the total cells were counted, and so two kinds of cells were differentiated. The whole system was embedded in the Leonard Skeggs invention of the bubble separated continuous flow technology that Technicon had already applied very successfully to clinical chemistry tests like blood sugar and at least another dozen tests. The tests were all parallel in bubbled flowing streams that ended in a simple photo sensor to measure the results. It was called Simultaneous Multiple Analysis. (The SMA line of products was already very successful and a good money maker.)

In the first week of my work I had a chance to talk with Len Ornstein. I expressed some concern for the fact that there were only two cell types differentiated, and that there were truly five types in the blood stream along with special cells related to leukemia. I also thought that for cells to eat iron particles they had to be live cells, and we had already committed to using three day old blood. In that case the cells may or may not still be alive. Len agreed that there was concern, and the two of us began to talk about an alternative project. It took about two weeks from the beginning to think it through to a possibility. Our idea was to use the existing publications of the international committee of hematology, known as the French American British (FAB) Committee who had shown that each of the common cell types could be identified under the microscope with a special histochemical stain. We would use these as "Markers" for each cell type, and make simultaneous multiple analysis in flowing streams. Len had already familiarized himself, in his laboratory with the microscope staining methods, except for the Basophil, which I knew already how to stain. So the task was to translate all the chemistry to a flowing stream and to make contrasts in a way that individual cell types can be counted as well as counting the total number of cells in the same flowing stream.

In the third week of my employment I made a memorandum to Hy Mansberg. The memo listed the concerns with the present project and proposed an alternative. But it did not give schedules or budgets. In retrospect, this was a foolish thing to do because I knew nothing of industrial cause and effect. I thought for a while that my memo had gone into an industrial never-never land. But in about a week Hy came back to me and said, "Alex, Jack liked your proposal. It is now your project. Bill Smythe (VP of R&D) and I want to review your needs and we would like to make a new budget for your project."

I was shocked! It had not been my intention to take over the project. And I suddenly had charge of a team of people who were hardly suited for the task that Len and I had in mind. But Hy Mansberg said we could redesign the personnel and that other company people could also be in and out of the project as was needed. In terms of management, Hy Mansberg was a very strong support and it was his mentoring that enabled me to focus on the science of the project.

In the next several weeks we defined and gradually hired personnel if not available. Here is one story just to indicate the size of the task. I needed an open minded medical technician who was not stuck on doing things like he or she had learned in the medical laboratories. It happened that the one most suitable from my interviews was a mini-skirt wearing young lady, Linda Racciopi. When I wanted to hire her

Bill Smythe, along with Hy Mansberg called me into an office and asked "Why do you want to hire a miniskirt?"

My answer was that I was trying to populate a project with a variety of talents, and that Linda had five of them. And I listed those talents. After that I was not questioned about whom to hire. But I did get a lot of help in interviewing and hiring the engineers. One of them was a long term friend and associate of Hy's, Jack Kusnets. He became a strong support throughout the whole project.

I also found that the various people in the project did not understand beyond their special fields and training. It took a long time to overcome this. But the method was clear. I started a weekly meeting at which one or more people described the progress and successes of their part of the project. It was expected that everyone should understand the reports. There was no stupid question, because the one asking may never have thought about that part of the discipline. I have to say that I asked my fair share of those questions, partly to understand engineering, in which I had no prior experience, and partly to manage the project. If there were big difficulties in understanding, we just took more time. It was not long afterwards that Hy came to me and suggested that we discontinue these meetings, The reason was that people in other projects looked in to what we were doing and said "Alex is running a country club."

In some ways it was true. But it was more a family atmosphere than a fun club. In one instance it did become family. Linda, met the love of her life, Mark Tatro, on the job. Mark was not a Catholic and that created problems for their wedding because her strict parish priest refused to have a wedding ceremony in his church. Linda came to me for help, and I found a priest for her who was more liberal. He had once given a sermon in the Tarrytown church about how he was an alcoholic. That the wine at Mass was his greatest temptation. And how he dealt with it. He was happy to perform the union. The reception afterward was giant, and must have been attended by half the Italians in New York State.

But we continued the meetings. And eventually the team became what in the trade is called "System Oriented." I learned much later that there are very few people in the field, let alone at our company, who had a system orientation. And just as a side comment, a considerable number of the team on the project later became vice presidents of R&D

or other responsibilities. In part it is because they were comfortable in the many areas of a complex system.

And indeed it was a complex project. Many of the areas we touched on were very new at the time, although they are now commonplace. The struggle to put them together had been in part a struggle to pull the team together. But beyond that, the science and engineering created quite a few new discoveries. It was decided that the basic biology inventions were to be patented at Mount Sinai. All the equipment orientation was to be patented by Technicon. All of these had my name as well as those others who contributed. And just as in academics I published the science in peer reviewed journals.

Four years later, the result was an SMA based device that did indeed classify 10,000 white blood cells with totally automated chemistry, flowing streams and self focusing streams passing a microscope type of sensor that always both counted all the cells that passed by at 2 meters per second, but also made sub – classification of the individual cell type by the special stain. And indeed we were able to do those classifications by the FAB classification. Thus the equipment was radically new in design but was based on classical and traditional medical knowledge.

The automation was so complete that some of the most successful salesmen would say to customers, "Doctor, you put the test tube of the patients blood at this end, then press the button and a printout comes at the other end. What happens in between is none of your business."

One memorable event was the first showing of our shiny new product at a Technicon International Show. The company held one of these shows every two years as a marketing venture. What I recall is standing in a large banquet hall at a podium in front of three thousand laboratory people and beginning my talk with:

"Automation in medical laboratories has the purpose of removing the operator from the tasks, making the tasks easier to perform and more efficient and also making the answers more accurate and precise than is otherwise possible. Today we present to you the automation of the differential white blood cell count."

I had fulfilled my personal promise. Before the day was over there were sixty purchase orders for this previously unknown equipment. Each order for $68,000.

I had also fulfilled a personal promise for Jack Whitehead. From the time he had taken the company over from his father he had the personal ambition to automate the "diff". There was an enormous mural in the entryway of his company headquarters depicting white cells as seen in a microscope. At the other side of the lobby there was a giant bubble machine that mechanically depicted the first technology that already had made megabucks for his private company. Jack had supported the effort to put these two ideas together.

One effect, of course, was that Jack took his company public very shortly afterwards. His comment at the time was, "Overnight I became a billionaire!" But Jack did not change in his ways at the company. He was a strict task master, with great expectations. I know many of his people who personally benefited form his disciplined approach to business. They often admit in private that Jack was directly the cause of their success in whatever they ventured to next.

The other effect of our automation was more difficult to accomplish. That was the acceptance of such a radically new device in the medical community. I saw the difficulty developing, and went to Dave Bishop, the senior Vice President of Marketing, and offered to help. It was agreed that I should spend a year reporting to Dave and build that acceptance. At the end of the year I was to go back to be the director of R&D for hematology. I thought it was a fair agreement.

I was given very free reign to do this task. I visited all the best known hematologists, and presented the new ideas both from an academic and a laboratory point of view. They were relatively easy to win over to the concept. But the next step was to have them sponsor evaluations. Surprisingly, they all agreed. Either they themselves, or people in their departments all took part, and eventually published peer reviewed papers on the new "Diff". One of the secrets in persuasion was that I was allowed to bring them together for discussions that fostered a common goal. They each contributed to what articles should be important to write. They all had giant expectations for the automated diff. And as the scene developed they were all satisfied. Meanwhile, at each such meeting, the marketing group were silent "flies on the wall" observing the reactions of these specialists. And after each meeting we spent hours discussing, explaining and interpreting.

Then I went beyond this group and had evaluators form various different kinds laboratories that could use the automation. It included the Mayo Clinic who came to us asking to do an evaluation. It also included the biggest commercial laboratory in the US at the time.

To give that as the example of the financial success of the "system", Metpath, in New Jersey, was at the time doing 2000 chemical analysis per night on their SMA chemistry systems. They were doing 600 microscopic differentials per night as "lost leaders". They did so because if they did not, then the doctors who sent their patients to Metpath would otherwise have sent them somewhere else. They purchased two of our Differential systems that could each do 60 samples per hour. One was to be a spare in case the other broke down, because once they had the workload it was a risk not to have the ability to perform. Within a month they purchased another two, because the work load had increased. Within three months they had purchased eight systems and were doing between 1000 and 1300 differentials per night! That was because they now made profit on the test and their sales force was actively selling it.

In the year of Marketing adventures I also traveled with individual sales people to help them develop an approach for this very new system. I have to say, I was not a good sales person myself. That was not the idea. But I did learn. For example, I once visited the laboratory chief at the Veterans hospital in San Francisco. The chief and his technician sat with us for over an hour and we had a wonderful discussion on the instrument and on academic hematology subjects. The salesman was with us and was listening. After another hour had passed and we were still at the same subjects, I stopped for a moment and said, "You know, we came visiting today to see if you would buy our new differential."

The doctor turned to me and said, "I thought I told you an hour ago that we want to buy one." Both I and the salesman had missed the cue! But the salesman was quick to respond. He got signatures, and walked the paper work through. We came away with a purchase order.

When I got back to Tarrytown, it was on an evening when Dave Bishop had his senior staff to dinner at a fancy restaurant. I was late to the dinner. Dave's first question to me was, "Did you get the order?"

My response was, "I don't take orders."

Dave said, " I have noticed that myself at times."

So then I told him that the salesman did get the order and was bringing it back himself. We did have a good relationship in the department.

Altogether I had 23 peer reviewed papers written in that one year. Some of them I mostly wrote myself for evaluators who were too busy to do the writing. Then I put them on the doctor's desk and asked, "is this what you intended to say about your evaluation?"

The most pleasing evaluation to me was one about showing that treatment of cancer was made much easier with the ability to follow the effect on white blood cells. We had come full cycle. And now it came clear to me that laboratory testing can and does save lives.

And then there was another Technicon international meeting at which there was now a hematology section of speeches. At that meeting I told Dave Bishop that I was leaving Technicon. I gave my paper that was the summary of all the technology and evaluations, and ended by listing all the people who had worked on the project. They were mostly all there and heard me call their names.

The reason I left was that I felt betrayed. Two weeks earlier I was told I would be going back to R&D but not to head the hematology group. I would have a nice laboratory where I could invent as much as I wanted. And I would report to one of the engineers whom I had trained on the project. It took less than a week of phone calls to get a job that had been offered to me by a competitor about a year earlier. In my mind a deal is a deal. I had done enough for Jack so that this treatment was not acceptable. Many years later he once privately admitted the error to me.

Other ventures

A LONG TIME LATER, while I was working at Becton Dickenson Company in the San Francisco Bay Area, in a discussion with the division president, Nagesh Mhatre he told me his very simple tests for any new project in the business of clinical laboratory testing. Likely these are the same tests that can apply to any new business venture. His grammar was somewhat influenced by his East Indian heritage. But the thoughts are very clear:

- Is it real?
- Can we do it?
- Can we win?

Each of these is a truly complex question. Reality involves not only the science but also the patentability of the concept and the medical arts surrounding the science.

Unfortunately the "we" in the last two questions does not always refer to the same people. Sometimes a private agenda will win when the whole project is bound to fail. If the private agenda is not obvious to all there may be people, and companies, hurt along the way. So it was with my next venture.

At a scientific meeting at Asylomar, in California, where I had been invited to talk about the automation of the differential, I was playing golf one free afternoon with Don Hart, who was head of one branch of regulatory affairs at Smith Klein at that time. He was associated with a small division of his company, called Geometric Data, that was developing a differential counter based on automating the slide based microscope. On the seventh hole tee, while we were waiting to drive, Don said to me, if I ever wanted to come work with that division, he knew they needed a vice president of R&D.

It was very simple to walk into that position. Its potential was also great, because the two products could very well complement each other. One was to do the high volume classification and flag abnormalities without diagnosing them. The other was to find the abnormal cells if they were there and assist the technologist in making actual diagnosis. Hence there would be screening and diagnosis as two different products. Indeed it was eventually purchased with that intent by the top laboratories, like the Mayo Clinic.

What I did not know was that Mel Miller, the division president and inventor of the technology, had his own agenda. It was very simple. All products developed for his company had to use his patented technology so he could get his royalties from all the products.   His patent was based on a very special type of pattern recognition. The claims included working with slides of blood samples stained by the conventional hematology stain. If the pattern recognition and the stain were not included he did not allow initiation of a product.

And so, when I designed his next product, the count of very immature red blood cells called Reticulocytes, the stain was not initially the one of his invention. I had to contrive a substitution stain to make it look the same. It worked anyway and it doubled the number of products in the company without changing the instrument platform.

Mel Miller also did not have in mind the second test of new products. "Can we do it?" He made commitments to the parent company on schedules without consulting his people, including me. Nor did he discuss the development of the product line with anyone besides the parent company.

Within a few years after I went there, Mel was let go from the company. And I got caught up in the same actions.   But I had made other contacts at Asylomar and at other meetings, and within a month of leaving Geometric Data I had a position at Becton Dickinson, in their California branches. This was a different task.   It was to pull together activities in two branches of a company that had common product potential, but were not able to talk to each other. I will tell that next. But first, I want to relate some other things that happened while at Geometric Data.

It was during my stay as VP of R&D at Geometric that the US government tried first to get involved in regulating laboratory medicine. Some US Senators, including Ted Kennedy, had come up with the idea to treat medical devices like drugs. The FDA was busy trying to put together a set of laws to govern medical devices. On one occasion all the players in the differential field were invited to a meeting called by a medical official. He told us that he had arranged to have all our products evaluated at his laboratory. We all had to supply our equipment and reagents and at least one technician. He then left the room to let us discuss a schedule.

The scientist from most companies were in favor of the idea, since they were confident of their equipment. The corporate representatives were very much against it. This included Mel Miller, who was as paranoid about individual company losers as any of the other players in the field. Mostly it seemed to the corporate representatives that the evaluation was not in their control. And if not in control then they could not be responsible. The decision was made that companies would not cooperate. But how should we state this. Mel Miller volunteered me to be the spokes person for the group. Most of the others knew me and they agreed.

When the official returned, I went to the white board at the front of the room and wrote on it, "It will not happen." And then I explained the concern for loss of control of such an evaluation. There was not much to do but accept our conclusion. This particular official had no more involvement in the process. But the FDA eventually agreed to have the companies prepare their own standards of performance and describe the methods of evaluation. I was involved in that committee, and wrote most of the statistical part of the evaluation. Years later there was a large meeting in a suburb of Washington DC where all the companies presented their evaluations according to the standard.

When the Food and Drug Administration eventually formed its laws and created advisory committees for various subjects, I was elected by the companies involved to be the industry representative to the hematology committee. Thus, for a short time I was the spokes person for the whole industry. It became an exposure to both diplomacy, patient explanation of both science and corporate interests, and at times giving difficult advice to corporations.

At one time a company made a presentation to the FDA committee. The mistake was to have the inventor of a device give the talk. When he was finished he was asked a question that was not directly on the subject as he understood it. His response was, "I could tell you the answer, but it is none of your business." The reaction was so strong that I eventually called for a coffee break and then privately advised the medical director of that company to withdraw his application and come back at another time. He did so and then presented with a more diplomatic staff member. They got their clearance.

And in such ways I discovered that it was necessary to contribute more than science in order to survive in the corporate environment. Here is just one more example of such an adventure.

One day Mel Miller called me to his office and said, " Alex, the president of our distributor company in Japan was having tea with the Secretary of Commerce. During the conversation he learned that Japan is responding to US criticism of not buying US goods. It is decided that two US manufactured goods are to be added to the list of government supported items. One of these is automated differential counters. Our distributor now has the name of 16 hospitals which are funded to make a purchase. What are we going to do?"

(I leave out the name of the distributor since it is a large company and I do not wish to betray his confidence. Also the other item on the list was Commercial Jet engines.))

Why Mel came to me I do not know because we had a perfectly good marketing department. But I answered, "Mel, that is easy. We will hold a symposium for our product. We shall invite the laboratory chief from each of the 16 hospitals along with his wife, girl friend and chief technician, (whether they are the same person or not). It will be for two full days and the agenda will include both detailed description of product and evaluators from both US and as many as possible from Japan. The prestige of mixing local and US evaluators will bring representatives from all the candidate hospitals."

Mel said, "Sounds good. What do you need?" It seems he had elected me to do the task.

"I need a presentable and informed person to whisper in my ear when the locals are giving their papers and during their discussions and to translate my product description and the US evaluators. The distributor must do everything else to prepare and invite all the guests, because we shall do this early next week if I can get at least one US evaluator to come."

And so it happened. The translator turned out to be highly informed and very presentable. She looked more like I had imagined the appearance of a geisha girl. Many of the doctors there had come with their cameras, and so I have a few pictures of this translator whispering in my ear! We had the top hematologist Professor Abbe, from Tokyo give the first local paper and he was very positive about his evaluation. He also became a good friend. All the doctors wanted to be my guide during the intermissions, and each one taught me the wonders of Sashimi, the local delicacy prepared by the first class caterer. The distributor had assigned one salesman to every three or four customers. And we kept score for the two days as to the number of purchase orders. By the end of the second day we had 12 of the 16 orders. We could have had the other 4 if the distributor would have agreed to assign a service person to that remote segment of Japan. But the distributor refused. Well, 75% of a $4,000,000 potential in five days is not a bad score for someone who does not take orders!

I had a great admiration for our Japanese distributor. But there are a few instances where the two cultures conflict and it is interesting to follow the interactions. On another visit to Tokyo I was asked to do a small diplomatic mission. I was asked to have Tea with Professor Abbe. That seemed simple enough. We sat at his academic Tea Room, on chairs out of courtesy to me. I and the professor faced each other in the middle, while two of the distributor managers were on either side of us at the table. In the middle of an academic discussion the professor stopped, and said,

"These distributors, you know, Dr. Saunders, make many diplomatic errors." He then went on to describe his grief by fact that his main competitor was also asked to evaluate the same instrument. During this brief tirade in the most serious tone the distributor managers were repeatedly bowing so deeply that their heads hit the tea table. They were in unison. Every time they were at the depth of their bowing, Professor Abbe looked across to me and winked. And that was it. The mission was highly successful.

There were only two real competitors at the time. But a lot of others were still trying.

Here is a brief summary of the industry at the time. I wrote this for the publications of the proceedings of the original evaluators meeting in Washington. (But it was not accepted by the peer review process. Hence this is its first publication.)

DOES IT MAKE A DIFFERENTIAL?
(Introduction to the NCCLS Conference on Differential Counts
11/20/84)   Recorded by Alex M. Saunders, M.D.

Listen, my children, and you shall hear,
Provided it's well reviewed by a peer,[1]
An account of science on a grand scale;
An account of business, bound not to fail;
Of government seeing beyond what is near;
Of discovery, finance and politics.[2] Dear
To so many for many a year.

Full of actors with high motivations
Who joined in this play from several nations.

The first is Jack,[3] who for two generations
Automated chemistry work stations.
Convinced by Leonard,[4] a friend from the past,
That another test was ready at last,
Gathered a team (very confidential)
To work on a White Blood Cell Differential.

And so it began with people who know
Engineering and math, and of course Leonard O.,
Whose knowledge of chemistry and of the cell
Continued to flow for a very long spell.

And so it began, indeed to be fair,
In two other corporate headquarters where
Other scientists, all in their prime,
Convinced the management that it was time.

---

[1] Scientific articles are usually submitted for peer review before
   acceptance by a journal. (This one was not well reviewed.)
[2] Business Week, Feb. 24, 1975, page 36.
[3] **E.C. Whitehead, Chai rman Technicon Instruments Corporation, 1968**
[4] Leonard Ornstein, Ph.D., Professor Pathology and Cell Research,
   Mount Sinai Medical School (1968).

Convinced them to take a shot in the dark.
Start a new project. (One was a LARC[5]
A Leukocyte Reading Computer they say;
With funding for forty man years and a day.)

To make this device will be a great feat.
Not one felt they had to compete.
Each project was highly confidential;
Who else would fool with a differential?

In one lab was Jim.[6] In another was Lou.[7]
Each highly confident, knew what to do:
Design a device somewhere in between
A microscope and a business machine.
Aided by Chuck,[8] abetted by Jean.[9]
Breadboards and patents. All of them clean.

Meanwhile in the West, at an early stage,
An endeavor on mice run by Leonard H.[10]
Reporting in private, sooner or later
The project will need a cell separator.
"Yes, single cells." declared the reporter,
Convincing Bernie[11] to build him a Sorter.

5   Bacus, J. Ph.D. Thesis. also: "Leukocyte Pattern Recognition."In :
     IEEE Transactions on System, Man and Cybernetics. SMC 2(4), 1972.
     (Became the basis of the Corning Medical LARC.)

6

7   Kamenski, L.,U.S. Patent # 413464, assigned to IBM.

8   Rogers, C.K. "Blood sample preparation for Automated Differential
     Systems." Am.J.Med.Tech.. 39: 435 442, 1973.

9   O'Brien, R. and Gotlieb-Rosenkrantz, P. "Studies of stained cell
     populations with the Rapid Cell Spectrophotometer." In: Automated
     cell Identification and Sorting (edited by G.L. Wied and G.F. Bahr.)
     Academic Press, New York, 1970.

10 **Hulett, H.R., Bonner, W.A., Sweet, R.G. and Herzenberg, L.A.**
     "Development and Application of a Rapid Cell Sorter." Clin. Chem.
     19(8): 813-816, 1973.

11 **Shoor, B., General Manager Becton Dickinson FACS Division, 1970.**

Ensuring that his dream will come true,
He also borrowed a machine from Lou.

As a guest in this lab Alex[12] was learning
A systems approach because he was yearning
To monitor each kind of Leukocyte
Very precisely while joining the fight
Against cancer of blood (and doing it right.)

Then musical chairs took a humorous bent.
The company gave Lou his patent.
A most fantastic business finesse,
He developed it into the R.C.S.
Rapid Cell Signals was his designation,
Which he sold to another corporation.[12]

Musical chairs sometimes are bizarre.
Leonard O., the original star,
With Alex and Jean once met in a bar.
Discovering that they shared the same dream
Recruited them onto Jack W.'s team.

And so it continues, with people who know
Cytochemistry and continuous flow;
Signal, noise and indexed refraction.
It was Leonard's brain and Alex's action.
A broadly based team doing their best
To turn whatever Jack would invest
(Each of four years a higher amount)
To a Differential Leukocyte Count
Automated. Then Jack with glee
Christened it the "Hemalog® D".

Jack did make one serious blunder.
An engineer, who with underground thunder,
Showed patterns in the way down deep

12   Saunders, A.M. and Hullet, R. Abstract to Histochemistry 5, 1966.

Of domes of oil in a million year sleep.
This fine engineer, Mel[13] was his name,
Concluded, he could use the same
Pattern techniques on cells, bright and dim,
In an interview when Jack showed them to him.

Designed on the train on his way back,
Mel christened it the "Hematrak®".
Arriving in Philly, he knew for sure,
Had already designed a three page brochure;
A prospectus as well.[14] Then Mel with glee
Sold it in town to a large company,
With a proviso that they consent
To keep him on as a president.

It is common in business to show brochures
Some time before the product matures.
This one was such. Here and there was a quirk.
(He asked Alex and others to make it work.)

But other companies did not dare
To enter the field without market share.
Rumors reaching the Street of Wall
Declared there were fourteen, in all,
Withdrawing from contest here and there.
Only the smaller ones showing despair.

Multiple corporate projects were few.
One company that everyone knew,
Over some time had more than two.

---

[13]   Ortho Diagnostics, a branch of J & J.

[13]   Miller, M US Patent Number _____

*   Just a note in passing. neither Jack, nor Mel, would ever "christen" anything, even with the best champagne. I will let you guess which one of them was a rabid Zionist.

[14]   Copy not available. Besides the brochure was not peer reviewed.

One was bought[15] , one developed[16], and one simply grew
Out of ambition and happenstance.
It really grew because of Resistance;
Or a more precise terminology
Is Electrical Resistivity[17]
On a small scale. Attaining the prize
Very simply by measuring size.[18]

Another venture used multiple dyes,
Some of them with energy transferred
To detectors, multiply sensored[19]
For a Block of time until the expense soared.[20]

The survivors, who had paid the price,
Each had to test their new device
Because it is not right to entice
Customers by just saying "It's nice."

At the very same time the thought occurred
In government circles, where names are blurred,
That all manufacturers could be thugs.

---

[15] Preston, K. "Computer Processing of Biomedical Immages." Computer 9(5):54 - 68, 1976.

[16] Arkin, C.F., Sherry, M.A., Gough, A.B. and Copeland, B.E. "An Automated Leukocyte Analyzer." Am. J. Clin. Path. 67: 159 - 169, 1977.

[17] Coulter, W. U.S. Patent #========, 1956. (Wallace Coulter produced the first effective cell counting device. This was a precursor for many of the differential counters that came later.)

[18] **Obergat, T.E., Zucker, R.M. and Cassen, B. "Rapid and reliable Differential Counts on Dilute Leukocyte Suspensions." J. Lab. and Clin. Med. 76: 518 - 522, 1970**

[19] Shapiro, H.M., Schildkraut, E.R., Curbelo, R., Turner, R.B., Webb, R.W., Brown, D.C., Block, M.J. "Cytomat - R: A Computer controlled multiple Laser source, multiparameter flow cytometer system." J. Histochem. Cytochem. 25: 836, 1977. (A joint venture between G.D. Searle and Block Engineering.)

[20] Curbelo, R., Schildkraut, E.R., Hirschfeld, T., Webb, R.H., Block, M.J., Shapiro, H.M. "A generalized Machine for Automated Flow Cytology System Design." J. Histochem. Cytochem. 23: 388, 1976.

Therefore to treat devices as drugs.
Pass a law, it is easy to do
If you ignore Jim, Alex and Lou.
Pass a law despite their invective.
"Devices must be SAFE AND EFFECTIVE."[21]

Even before this law ended hearing
One official became endearing
By asking each company to install
Their device in a government hall,
And under his own directive
Attest that they were safe and effective.

Hereby lay a corporate blunder;
They all buried this grand plan under
Heaps of memos. None willing to bend.
It was not the money they would not spend.
What turned each corporate heart to stone
Was fear of their losing this trial alone.
It did not come to pass in spite
The general concept of it was right.

The missing ingredient in this mess
Became known as "Consensus process."[22]
To overcome individual fears
Took the better part of ten more years.

Instead of joint trials, consensus dared
To write a standard on knowledge shared
By business, clinics and government,
All believing the time well spent.
Following the official directive
To prove devices safe and effective.

---

[21] Device Legislation sponsored by T. Kennedy and others was signed
    into law on May 28, 1976.
[22] National Committee for Clinical Laboratory Standards. "Tentative
    Standard, Leukocyte Differential Counting." Vol. 4, No. 11, 1984.

The list of actors has not abated.
Their work has recently been collated,[23]
And a three day meeting instigated.[24]
Indeed they have been dedicated.

The story's not ended. But is all true.
We have each sought something else to do.
Most of us have more than one invention,
And some have found market attention.
We like to tinker with something new.
Sometime soon I'll report more you.

Just a little side note:

The manufacturer who was involved in "more than two" was Coulter Electronics. Wallace Coulter was another hero of this whole story because he had created a simple cell counter, not a differential, much earlier than anyone else in the field. His patent was 1956, and so his involvement was as old as my dream of getting involved. He entered the hematology field years before Technicon, but his technology was not as amenable to doing the whole differential.

One day while I was in my marketing office at Technicon I answered my phone and a man at the other end said, "Do you know about the Coulter Counter?" I said "Yes, it is in competition with one of my companies products." He came back with, "Do you want to buy it?"

He wanted to sell me the plans for Wallace Coulter's newest products! I said, "Maybe. Call me back in an hour."

In moments I was in Jack Whitehead's office with Dave Bishop. In one breath Jack was on the phone to Wallace Coulter. Together we agreed to catch the thief. Wallace Coulter sent his brother, Joe, with

---

[23] The F.D.A. contracted with A.D. Little and Co. to produce a bibliography of automated differential counters. It contained well over 300 references to method, evaluations and clinical relevance.

[24] This meeting was sponsored by the National Committee for Clinical Laboratory Standards in November of 1984. It was chaired by John Koepke M.D., one of the earliest clinical evaluators of an automated differential. There were 25 speakers and an expert audience of over 100. Proceedings are published by Blood Cells, Springer Verlag

the named price of $100,000. We enticed the thief to a hotel room near the New York airport. I was there, wired with a recorder, when he was arrested while counting the money. And I testified at his trial.

That evening Joe Coulter invited me to the best dinner I ever had in my life.

More adventures

I HAVE HAD THE good fortune to be in projects from the very beginning. I mean, to plan the technology and to then carry the projects to completion. Having done this several times I was later invited to more of the same. And each time is a different set of circumstances and a different thrust. Often the circumstance is that there is a base technology and it is crying for one more money making application. What has been true pleasure is to combine that corporate desire with my own drive to bring a meaningful and needed product to market, and help the medical community to understand and to use the same. In many cases there was a fore-runner in the company who had a vision related to the need. I hope that these people with vision had as much pleasure in working with me as I had working with them or for them.

At Becton Dickinson it was Bernie Shoor. Bernie was the mover behind the creation of the Fluorescence Activated Cell Sorter (FACS). He had built it as a favor to Leonard Herzenberg, for his basement lab at Stanford. But it was Bernie who recognized the commercial value in research for being able to separate cell types according to their immunological characteristics. And thus he started a business division of BD for that purpose.

In short order BD also stated a division that manufactured the immunological reagents that could be used with the FACS. Eventually Bernie became president of both divisions and they became good profit centers for the parent company. Then Bernie began to dream of clinical applications of these reagents and instruments. He was looking for another division of the company to do the clinical applications. It so happened that I called him to say I was available just at the time when he was convincing the parent company to follow this lead. He had me interview a number of the top brass and then together we defined a new positioning in a new division called Clinical Cytometry.

The whole idea was to take the main technology of both divisions and combine into acceptable clinical products. The time was just right, because the type of cells to be identified had great application in the AIDS conditions that were then in a growth period. I had few resources and just one laboratory. But I had access to both divisions. So I took time and learned both technologies.

What became clear was that by catering to the researchers everything was too detailed and too sophisticated. It all had to be reduced to simple concepts and easy performance. There was to be no thinking about the results. Medical technologists do the same routine all the time and report the results. If something did not work, they are to call the manufacturer. It had to be foolproof.

Of course that did not mean the devices or reagents were to be simple. Quite the opposite is true. To make a device simple for the user meant to hide the sophistication. It meant that the sorting became redundant, but the instrument still had to recognize and identify with as much sensitivity. The reagents were coupled in such groups that the logic sorted out the cell kinds. No expert scientist was needed to interpret the results. There was a simple printout.

The patent office eventually agreed that there was new invention in all of this and granted some four new patents. Then the trick was to show the FDA that the tests were not new, but were substantially equivalent to prior marketed tests. That was a balancing act.

To go on, not every project I started turned into a successful result. There was, for example the major player in the microchip testing industry. The president of the company wanted to get into a medical field. It seemed logical to him that his large inspection microscope and automation should have use in a hospital setting. I spent some months studying his technology and made some proposals. They were, again, to simplify the mechanics to make them usable by medical technicians. And then apply them to a medical diagnostic field. We got stuck on a definition of "Can we win?" The concept of smaller equipment had no appeal whatever. Each unit should cost at least $1mm to $1.5mm. And there was no way to convince the two top people that hospitals did not buy into that temperament.

There is no need to describe in detail still more adventures. Only one is of interest because of the way science and business interacted. As I said before, the answer to the test question, "Can we win?" is different to different people. I will not name the company, and only say that it no longer is an independent entity. The founder was an engineer, and he built a business around a pattern recognition microscope. It became a stable business with a slowly growing customer base, and almost no reagent business. To grow his business he decided to start a new product line that had more reagents and also ended using the pattern recognition microscope technology. He had a project defined. It was a truly exciting project. He hired a search firm to find the project leader and she invited me to join this company. I agreed that if the funds were there the project passed all three criteria. The answer about funds was, "We plan to make a public offering as soon as the project looks feasible. And then we can easily finish the project."

What I was not told was that the president of the company defined "Can we win?" as making the public offering from which he could make his financial "win", and that he had an exit strategy. He had chosen me because of a track record, and especially because I had played a part in bringing another company public. I will only say that I did the design for him. It was the four new patents that convinced the underwriters to complete the Initial Public Offering. The exit strategy was to lose interest in the project. It was assigned to another person to complete, and was assigned to an inexperienced person to put through the regulatory cycle with the FDA. She managed to antagonize the FDA officials and the project never came on the market. In this case there was only one winner. I forgot to mention that he was even more of a Zionist than Mel Miller. In fact he took his money and ran to new life in Israel.

At the 45th anniversary of our graduation from medical school we had a reunion. There were both parties like we used to have and a scientific session where a number of us gave talks. I gave a talk with the title "This is my blood." In it I described the design and results of the tests that I have helped to put on the market. I made reference to Mac Whitelaw, whose cancer treatment project first got me interested in laboratory improvement. I also made reference to Hal Taylor who first got me interested in Histochemistry. And I showed the results of running my own blood sample in all the tests I brought to market.

It was not only my blood. It had become my life.

Religion, Business and Science

IN HOPES THAT I may be forgiven, I present this one chapter of free opinions. Here I give a different side of my personal story. It serves also to fill in a puzzle about how scientists position themselves in a world artificially divided between those who "have religion", and those who do not. And I try to cover why religion fails the current business environment. In many ways, science is also a business!

Because the best boarding schools were run by Catholic organizations I graduated from high school with a truly solid foundation in the Christian religion. These schools hold as their right to teach both academic subjects and their choice of religion with discipline and an expectation of excellence. In such a school one graduates not only with an understanding of one's career choices, but also with a clear vision that religion is part of ones whole future life.

And so it happens, that just as I have tried to keep up with science in general, and more specifically with my chosen fields by reading and by personal interactions, I have also tried to continue my personal and spiritual growth by reading and by personal interaction. Here, now, is a perspective that hopefully does not upset too many people.

On a social level, the Jewish bible holds up leaders as Priest, Prophet or King. Christians, and Catholics in particular, declare that one must take all three roles. And that all people must be all three. The key words here are "or" and "and". Neither point of view, in my opinion, is correct with the way society is presently constructed.

The concept of King is one in which there is a clear leader and an implied society of followers. The king rules by authority and the followers willingly give that authority. In the primitive, formative, years of Jewish history the priest was the one who knew and expressed the Law. Law was both social and religious. No distinctions were made and no line drawn. Questions as to God's law were not allowed. Thus the ban on eating pork, that obviously had a health implication, and the keeping of the Sabbath for God, are part of the same law. The Law was one of the balancing features, presenting the king with accepted restrictions. Prophets were people who more clearly saw the signs of the times. Because they did so consistently and independent of obligation to respond to these signs, they were respected for their warnings, but not always followed.

Even with the implication that their observations came from God, who used prophets as His conduit, prophets did not always succeed. Their "prophesies" were another balance on social power. But the growing, general, population of this primitive society, accepting their priest, prophets and king, were not any of these. Nor would the society have survived if everyone thought they were king.

The realistic exception to a population of followers was the Jewish mother. She, at times, was all three types of leader, and continues to be so today. I cannot say exactly how that works.

One learns to become a leader when others obviously show dependence. Then a choice is made. Is this a pleasing set of affairs? If pleasing, one takes on the attitudes and practice of leadership in more and more aspects of life. And people follow willingly. I personally learned the leadership role at the YMCA summer camp. The campers under my charge expected me to lead their activities. It included all daily activities and a role of inspiring these youngsters to achievements they had thought impossible when they came into my charge. I liked the role, learned to use it, but was not enamored by it.

As I grew out of the years at a Catholic institution I continue to perceive a need for sound social and religious experience in my life. Experience at the Newman Club during university days was very positive in this respect. But then the institutional part suddenly stopped. Attending church on weekends continues as a routine, but is less than inspiring on the whole. There is a simple reason for this. But it is difficult to explain politely.

Here is personal explanation that sometimes works. It is the simile of language to religion. When I left Hungary I stopped using the Hungarian language consistently. There were no demands on me to continue reading and speaking the language and hence my Hungarian grammar and vocabulary are those of an eight year old child. Indeed we recently visited Cousin Krisztina in Budapest. She took us to a picnic attended by her friends whom I had not met before. One very polite person told Krisztina that if he did not know better he would have thought me "retarded" because I spoke as an eight year old. And so it is with religion. Catholic institutions do a great job through the eighth school grade. Thereafter there are no real demands. The learning process stops. And essentially the whole flock of church goers becomes retarded in religious growth. The potential adult richness of the religious experience never happens to the "person in the pews."

In this one instance, I shall assign blame. And then also exonerate. Parish priests have a choice within their own parish on how resources are to be spent. Those resources include their own personal skills. They can decide to address themselves to the needs of adults, or to the needs of the next generation. Or they may decide that by addressing the needs of adults they may leave the needs of the next generation to the adults to whom he responds. For many priests it becomes far easier to respond to the needs of children. Adults are helped only with the same needs as they had when they were children. Hence as Christians, Catholic adults become retarded, unless they use their own resources. These resources must come from their training in the many fields of modern society. That also may be acceptable, except for the fact that the Catholic Church discourages independent thought.

As a scientist, I find myself listening to a pep talk type of sermon, and applying my scientific discipline to what I hear. I may question a simple-minded concept that is not consistent with experience. But it is not possible to request clarification as one would do at a lecture or seminar. And so it is up to me to look up an answer, or to do further reading, if I have time.

I estimate that at least 70% of the people in the pews (at least in my parish) have educational levels above that of the priest. Not only those in the sciences, but practically all upper education, emphasizes rules of consistency and habits of questioning inconsistency when presented. The result of not getting answers to those questions is the major cause of retardation in just the religious growth of the population, while the same population continues to grow in many other aspects of their lives. The tragedy is that it need not be so.

I shall explain how I reach this conclusion. On two occasions, like bible study classes, I did an experiment in our parish. I took a strong leadership role, by doing deep research into the fields and then expressing opinions with clear confidence in the sessions. The remainder of the group sat back and became dependent on a "leader". They were eager to learn and glad that someone would do this for them. The sessions ended, and I backed away. This is not my career. And as I watched, the leadership role remained empty of intellectual content.

However it is not the fault of the priest. He is only the product of his training, and the expectation that within his own parish he becomes king without any training to be king. The difficulty is that in becoming king often he is no longer priest. He is no longer the one required to pass on the rich traditions of the Law. Most often he has not become a prophet in the sense of seeing the signs of the times. But he is still expected also to speak in the name of God and make it relevant. Very few can respond to this expectation. In my lifetime I have known four. One is no longer a priest. None of the rest was trained in the diocese where I now live.

My own need is met by admitting to myself that the Judeo Christian religion has its basis in a primitive society. Until the arrival of the Christian Era this society grew and succeeded by not questioning the rules. Then there was a brief period of questioning and then a relapse with no consistent critical review for another two millennia.

Here is an example; God, through the mouth of prophets and writers advises primitive society to increase and multiply. It was indeed good for primitive society to do so, for their own protection. We now have filled the face of the earth and are still advised by the same book to increase and multiply. I can see the signs of the times have changed. But I am not the prophet to force a new perspective on the whole community. Prophets who are doing so now have as hard a time bringing about change as did Jeremiah of old.

> The problem with one Jeremiah
> Was to convince his King, Zedekieah,
> That Egyptian gold And idolaters, bold,
> Will bring down brimstone and fire.

Repeating his message again
And repeating always in vain,
He was thrown down a well   Because he would yell
"All Jerusalem's down the drain!"

Wherever prophets may go
Their credibility's always low.
Their call is for action. There is no satisfaction
In saying, "I told you so."
        The Bible in limericks By Alex M Saunders, MD

I also view the religious community with the needs of a business person. I read more than a dozen Parables, which are also part of the liturgy read on Sundays. Each parable shows that the founder of our religion knew the practices of business people of his day. He speaks about hiring and firing. He speaks about budgeting, planning and the effects of inadequate planning,   He speaks about the vagaries of competition, about ethics, cheating and use of personal influence to achieve unfair advantage.   Although these gospel readings are a frequent occurrence on Sundays, the topics I just mentioned are never the subject of weekend preaching. Yet these are exactly the concerns we, in business, meet every day. And we need an adult perspective for our weekday activities. Instead we are told that we spend the week doing "godless things" and then do not understand most of the weekend worship we attend.   Truly, it is the other way around.   I expect my weekend inspiration to help me when I am about to fire a person on Monday morning. I may expect even more support on Sunday if I was, myself, fired on Friday evening. And if I am prepared for these happenings of the real world I may cope with them better, and even make better decisions when business, morals and ethics are in conflict.

In the converse, the experience of the business community could be of great service to the Church. Understanding the marketing aspects of filling needs, for example, would greatly benefit continuity and growth in a parish. Instead when that offer is made, priests respond that "marketing is a dirty word". The tragedy is that the priest believes what he said. That is how he is trained.

It is even more amusing when we hear Catholic bishops complain about Catholic politicians voting without regard to "Church Teaching". But the same bishops have refused to educate those politicians on a weekly basis on exactly the same subjects, long before they come up for a vote.

These are the signs of the times. Oh well!

And so, with the critical training obtained through a disciplined Catholic education, and later scientific training, I have my own synthesis of religion and science. This synthesis leaves out the authority of priest, prophet and king. Of course the main issue must be how to reconcile inconsistency. I simply start by accepting the discipline of thought provided in science. I follow this by gathering of facts, and then evaluate inconsistencies. I also start by recognizing that the foundation of religion, on which the rest is built, is our bible. The various books have different authors, intent, and literary style. It is here that discipline of analysis helps.

Some books begin with repetition of myths. I do not mean that to be derogatory, so I shall explain. A myth is a happening re-told and re-interpreted, and often re-distilled over the course of pre-history and historical times. Of necessity the interpretation is in context of knowledge of the day. Some examples of obvious myths and their origin are easy to discover.

Noah's flood is related to the pre-historical re-filling of the Mediterranean ocean, or was it the Caspian Sea, at the end of the last ice age, as the oceans rose and spilled into these basins. There is good geological evidence for both of these happenings. The morality story built into the biblical account is of more interest to bible readers than the idea of accepting Noah as a historical figure.

The story of Jonah and the great fish only makes sense if Jonah began his journey in the neighborhood of Ur, in the delta of the Tigris and Euphrates rivers. There was no waterway from Palestine to the Arabian Gulf at that time. The story is a non historical re-telling of a tribal migration up the Euphrates river, past Nineveh and settling first in the region where towns are named for the family of Abraham. Harran, for example, was the father of Abraham, and also the name of a town in upper Euphrates, where Abraham is said to have settled before he went to Palestine. The town is still on the map today.

Destruction of Sodom, Gomorrah and Jericho are based on real destruction of Palestinian towns by earth quakes. All of Palestine sits on an earth quake fault. The archeological evidence for towns repeatedly destroyed and rebuilt is very strong. However there is no good archeological evidence for towns with hundreds of thousands of people in the Palestinian region at the time of Joshua. Hence the book of Joshua, with its account of destructions of such hundreds thousands of soldiers must have a different intent than history. Conquering the peoples of Palestine was more likely by providing the substance of civilization and by the law of survival of the fittest. A matter of choice of tribes to become unified over time was emphasized by Joshua's speech that he chooses the Lord in preference to the religion of his ancestors who came across the river. That river is the Euphrates, not the Jordan that he had just crossed.

The origin of these stories in myth only speaks to the low probability of their historical nature as written. The principle that is more difficult to understand and to accept is that God does not interfere with history. The Jewish bible converts my examples so that God plays active roles in each. He directs the migration to Palestine, He destroys the resistance to Jewish population of the land. And He does so in the cause of both morality and nurturing of "His People." That sounded good in context of the time. It was an essential component of building a more mature nation whose cohesive force is their religion.

Following this reasoning, there is no concern with admitting that the remainder of Genesis is non historical. Hence there is no concern about trying to reconcile the theory Evolution with the naming of creatures in the Garden of Eden. On the other hand, creation is a reality. One cannot deny existence of a Creator. Science is merely the organized study of creation.

Of course, not all books of the bible are myth. And the analysis of how written and for what context is the substance that must be researched and integrated if one is to find answers. It would be great if organized religion continued to do this with professionally trained authorities, and then provide that information to the "people in the pews". There are a lot of professionally trained people doing the work, as one can discover by research, but they never connect with the people in the pews.

I said that I believe that God does not interfere with history. However I do believe that at one time, about 2000 years ago God

Do we need to explain?

ABILITY TO THINK for the benefit of others may be the highest form of human development. Peter Paul did so for corporations he founded and led, and for numerous corporations that invited him to their boards of directors. This included a bank, a trust company and an insurance corporation. He had the ability to discern future needs of his community, and took action. He was a founder of businesses to fill those needs, including Vancouver's Television station, and the ski complex on Grouse Mountain. The fact that these also returned benefit to him is part of his skill. But it was not always a requirement. He played giant roles in support of the Art Gallery, the Arthritis Foundation and long before he was a patient he was the president of the Canadian Cancer Society. And there is much more.

Over the 51 years of their marriage, Peter Paul discovered a hobby that he and Nancy could enjoy together. It was the planning of their beautiful homes. Nancy shared his drive for perfection, and indeed, with his encouragement, she designed and built a vacation home that is both beautiful and perfectly livable. And that is what they both enjoyed to the full; to live in the environments that they had created. That environment included their personalities. And their children.

A previous chapter describes how Frank fit into the same category; someone who is able to think for the benefit of others. My two brothers were very different, yet here was a common meeting ground.

As for me, the health and life saving benefits to others were always a priority. Along the way I learned to merge corporate success with scientific endeavor. Whatever I have done was always with cooperation, inspiration and strong support from Peggy, my wife. Our story is not finished. Peggy and I are still busy. Both projects and the pleasure of our children and grandchildren still occupy us fully.

The story about the Pearly Gates in my introduction comes back to mind. My two brothers have now passed that way. Who knows how St. Peter measures the credits and debits of one's life?

The book you have just read is to our credit.

The poetry sprinkled throughout the book explains why I wrote it. At the death of my mother, I was too young to grieve for her.

> There was no time for grieving,
> No time to know my mind
> I just knew ……………..

At the death of my brothers, some seventy years later, I was still not able to show my grief as I should have, and yet;

> I do not write for your belief.
> I write just to relieve my grief.